LONGING AND LIES

This Large Print Book carries the
Seal of Approval of N.A.V.H.

LONGING AND LIES

DONNA HILL

THORNDIKE PRESS

A part of Gale, Cengage Learning

GALE
CENGAGE Learning™

Detroit • New York • San Francisco • New Haven, Conn • Waterville, Maine • London

GALE
CENGAGE Learning™

LIBRARY OF CONGRESS CATALOGING-IN-PUBLICATION DATA

Hill, Donna (Donna O.)
    Longing and lies / by Donna Hill.
        p. cm. — (Thorndike Press large print African-American)
    TLC (The Ladies Cartel Series, # 4)
    ISBN-13: 978-1-4104-2417-4
    ISBN-10: 1-4104-2417-0
    1. African Americans—Fiction. 2. Women private investigators—Fiction. 3. Infants—Crimes against—Fiction. 4. Large type books.
    I. Title.
    PS3558.I3864L66 2010
    813'.54—dc22   2010009311

Published in 2010 by arrangement with Harlequin Books S.A.

I sincerely have to thank my editor
Glenda Howard who has the patience
of a saint! Many thanks to the readers
who have embraced the TLC series
and shared their enthusiasm with
their friends.

Dear Reader,

Welcome to my latest novel in The Ladies Cartel series. Hopefully, you've already met Savannah, Danielle and Mia, fierce sisters. This time I will introduce you to my most complex character, Ashley Temple.

You may remember her from *Temptation and Lies* as Mia's assistant. Now she has her own story, one that is timely and ripped right out the pages of today's headlines. But what is a romance without the hero? Have I got a hero for you! Elliott Morgan. Tall, dark, mysterious, handsome and wickedly sexy. Of course he has his flaws. But we can work with him!

I'm a little sad to part with my ladies as *Longing and Lies* is the last book in the series. Hopefully, Savannah, Danielle, Mia and Ashley will turn up on the pages of some of my other romances, keeping readers up to date on what's happening with them. I do hope that you have enjoyed each one: *Sex and Lies, Seduction and Lies* and *Temptation and Lies.*

I want to thank you for picking up this book, trying it out and hopefully enjoying it as much as I enjoyed writing it. It is because of your support that I have been able to bring book after book to readers for the past twenty years! Amazing.

Thank you for all that you do for me. Happy reading.

Donna

CHAPTER 1

The month of April had definitely lived up
to its reputation. For a solid week, it rained
in every variety from bad-hair-day mist to
outright downpours complete with thunder
and lightning.

Ashley Temple sent up a prayer of thanks
as she pulled back her bedroom curtains to
usher in the first rays of sun in a week. She
stretched catlike, raising her face to the
warm rays that beamed through the window.

The previous week had been difficult for
more reasons than bad weather. She'd
recently finished up an assignment where
she'd had to pose as a college coed to break
up a drug-trafficking operation on campus.
She developed friendships with some of the
girls that she ultimately had to turn in. She
could still see their faces, the looks of
betrayal, the hurt and terror in their eyes.

She sighed heavily and turned away from
the new day. There were times when she

wished that The Cartel was not part of her life. As a member of the secret organization, she could never have a real life, because part of who she was and what she did could never be revealed to anyone outside of The Cartel's inner circle. That fact alone limited forming any long-lasting intimate relationships. And as she crept past the age of thirty, the desire to find someone and something permanent was beginning to fill her thoughts more each day.

However, there were some wonderful benefits. She'd met some of the most incredible women through The Cartel and forged unbreakable friendships. Savannah, Mia, Danielle and more recently Traci, were the savviest sisters she'd ever met. Somehow they'd all managed to maintain the man in their lives, get married or engaged, have kids and still kick major butt when duty called. So there was definitely hope for her at the end of the "espionage rainbow."

She was closest to Mia, having worked as her assistant at MT Management — Mia's event-planning firm — for the past year and being a shadow on Mia's last assignment that involved an elite illegal escort service. That assignment had been harrowing at best, testing the ladies on many levels, but it had been nothing compared to MT Management's crème de la crème affair, the coordination of the triple wedding ceremony for three of The Cartel members: Claudia and Bernard, Mia and Steven and Danielle and Nick. Although they'd all returned back to work, they were still gooey-eyed and bubbly. If she didn't like them all so much, it might just turn her stomach.

Ashley turned away from the window, sat down on the side of the bed and put on her sneakers. She wasn't expected at the office until ten, and she wanted to get in her morning run before the streets grew too crowded with the mad dashers en route to work in bustling Manhattan.

She loved the city, she thought, stepping outside and taking a deep breath of rain-washed air, particularly the eclectic atmosphere of lower Manhattan where she'd lived for the past five years. It was a mixture of young and old, exciting and sublime, from mom-and-pop stops to reservations-only restaurants. The aroma of foods from around the world wafted through the air, giving the city its own unique, and often mouth-watering scent.

Ashley did a few stretches on the front steps of her four-story apartment building before slowly taking off down Avenue A. She waved to Herbie as she jogged by his newsstand, making a mental note to pick up a paper on her way back and a lottery ticket. She was no more than three blocks from her apartment when the vibration went off on her hip. She glanced down at the illuminated screen of her BlackBerry. "Anonymous." She knew exactly who it was.

Ashley circled the block in her tan 2000 Honda Accord before finding a parking space on 126th Street, across the intersection from TLC's headquarters.

As she walked down the street, she was continually amazed at the gentrification that had taken place in Harlem over the last decade and even more so in the past two years. It was almost unrecognizable except for the tree-lined blocks that still embraced the stately brownstones, many of which had been restored to their former glory, when Harlem was in vogue and the salons were frequented by Langston Hughes, Adam Clayton Powell and the like discussing the "Negro condition."

Ashley reached her destination and spotted several well-toned guys entering a brownstone, which was actually the Pause for Men Day Spa, owned by four women. She'd had the opportunity to meet them and visit the spa on several occasions and was totally impressed with what they had accomplished. And with The Ladies Cartel headquarters tucked unobtrusively across the street, it was a testament to the power of women on this stretch of street in Harlem.

Ashley approached the brownstone. To the casual observer, TLC headquarters was simply another restored brownstone that ran the Tender Loving Care body products business, which would account for the traffic of women and the often large, all-female gatherings. However, it was anything but that.

She rang the bell and moments later Claudia answered the door. Claudia was Jean's right hand and long-time TLC operative. What was most intriguing was that she was Savannah's mother, and it had been Claudia who recruited her own daughter into the organization, and in turn Savannah brought in Mia and Danielle.

"Hello, sweetheart," Claudia greeted, clasping Ashley's shoulders and kissing her cheek. "You look stunning and stylish as always," she said, taking in Ashley's wild, spiral afro, knee-high brown suede boots over a pair of very tight jeans, layered T-shirts and a thick, brown leather belt hanging low on her slender hips.

13

Ashley grinned. "Thanks." She stepped in. "How's married life?"

Claudia beamed. "Wouldn't have it any other way."

"Don't wear Bernard out with your bad self," Ashley teased.

Claudia made a face. "Now where's the fun in that?"

They both laughed.

"Jean is waiting for you," she said as they approached the stairs. "You should be very proud of yourself."

Ashley looked at Claudia over her shoulder. Her brow creased. "Proud of myself? Why?"

"Jean rarely picks the same operative for assignments back-to-back." She smiled slowly. "She thinks very highly of you."

For an instant Ashley's stomach tensed. The corner of her mouth flickered. "I guess that's a good thing. Huh?"

Claudia merely smiled and turned away.

Ashley drew in a breath, turned and headed up the stairs to Jean's office on the second floor. As she went up she passed the Hall of Fame that held the pictures of many of the TLC operatives on the wall, hers included. She made a mental note to give them an updated photo. One of the most recent additions was Brenda's

14

picture — the prodigal daughter — who'd returned to the fold during Mia's last assignment.

She went up the next flight and down the hall, tapped lightly on Jean's partially opened door.

"Come in."

Ashley stepped inside and was surprised to see Bernard sitting in the office, as well. Bernard Hassell, Claudia's husband, was Jean's connection to Homeland Security, the FBI and CIA. Bernard's influence ran so deep into that side of government that it was a little scary. None of the TLC members wanted to know what he really did. It was simply better not to. Other than that, he was a great guy and a dead ringer for Billie Dee Williams.

"Please have a seat," Jean instructed as she took off her signature red-framed glasses.

Jean Wallington-Armstrong — although she rarely used her married name — was at that magic point in her life where she could have been thirty or fifty. She was in excellent physical shape, known to jog four miles a day and workout in the gym three times a week. Her skin was still smooth with a light sprinkle of freckles across her nose. Her arresting green eyes didn't miss a trick and her lustrous red hair glowed with vitality. She could easily be mistaken for the actress that played Addison on *Grey's Anatomy* before moving on to star in *Private Practice.* But most of all it was the power that Jean exuded, from her commanding presence to her no-nonsense attitude that mesmerized everyone who met her, which was why it was so hard to believe that any man could have gotten away with hurting her emotionally — like her ex-husband did. At least that was the urban legend that circulated around The Cartel. No one spoke about it outright, but there were whisperings, especially when Brenda returned. But that was another story.

"Bernard, good to see you."

He nodded his head. "You, too. Congratulations on the high school case. Great job."

"Thanks," she murmured. She took a seat opposite Jean.

Jean opened a folder then looked across the wide oak desk at Ashley. "The reason I asked Bernard to join us is that he is going to be involved from the beginning."

Ashley rested her oversized purse on her lap, crossed her ankles and waited. That was an interesting twist, she thought. Bernard usually brought up the rear or came on board when things got a bit dicey. So to have him involved from day one put her on alert.

"There has been a rash of children that have gone missing. Babies, infants. Some of them from their homes or right from the hospital never to be seen again. The government is keenly aware of this." She flashed Bernard a look.

"But with a war on two fronts, the weak economy and a host of other national and world issues, they don't have the manpower to tackle this the way it needs to be tackled," Bernard said.

As they talked, explaining her assignment, Ashley fought down the nausea that brewed in her stomach. Her temples pounded and she felt the beads of perspiration lining her forehead and trickling down the center of her spine. She took in short breaths to steady her stomach as her heart thundered in her chest. Why her? Why did they pick her for this? Oh, God. Her throat clenched.

"We will need you to infiltrate several of these agencies," Jean was saying, cutting into Ashley's twisting emotions. "We think that is the best starting place. These agencies serve as the conduit from the places of abduction to the buyers. We're just hoping that these children have not been taken out of the country."

Ashley rubbed her damp palms along her thighs.

"Are you all right, Ashley?" Jean asked.

Ashley's gaze snapped toward Jean. She swallowed. "Yes. I'm fine. Just thinking . . . how horrible it must be for the parents."

Jean looked at her for a moment before continuing. "We decided that the best cover for this assignment is for you to have a partner."

"A partner?" she echoed.

Bernard cleared his throat. He turned to Jean. "May I?" Jean nodded for him to go ahead. He leaned backward and folded his arms. "We need to ensure from the onset that your cover is tight. To do that we decided that it was best that you be part of a couple."

"A couple?" she repeated for lack of something concrete to say.

"Yes."

Jean opened a folder and adjusted her glasses on the bridge of her aquiline nose. "The FBI is part of this operation. I asked Bernard to go through the files and select the agent that would be best suited for this. His name is Elliot Morgan. He's just returned from an operation overseas."

"I've already briefed him on what needs to be done," Bernard added. "And he's agreed."

Ashley adjusted herself in her seat.

"He should be here shortly, but we wanted to speak with you first. So if you have any reservations, now is the time to let me know," Jean said.

Ashley cleared her throat. "I've just never worked with a male operative before," she said, looking from one to the other.

"Under normal circumstances we try to tailor all of our assignments for Cartel members only. But this is a highly sensitive case. In addition to which, the FBI wants to be involved."

Ashley nodded. The knot of tension tightened in her stomach. Did Jean know about that dark, painful part of her life? Is that why she was selected for this assignment?

There was a light knock on the door.

"Come in," Jean called out.

All heads turned in the direction of the opening door.

CHAPTER 2

Elliot Morgan's trained dark eyes took in the room and its occupants all at once. He was still tense and edgy from his undercover assignment in London where he was on the trail of a serial bomber. His senses remained on high alert, expecting the unexpected at any moment. In his shady world where no one was who they claimed to be, everyone was suspect. He'd seen more in his thirty-six years than most people had in a lifetime.

Ashley's breath stopped somewhere in her chest and wouldn't budge. The new arrival had virtually sucked up all the air in the room. Tall, dark, athletically muscular, he brought to mind the sleekness and danger of a predatory panther. His features were hard and chiseled with deep probing eyes and full lips. His closely shaven hair was more of a shadow than anything else. But it was more than his physical presence that was breathtaking. It was clear by the way he moved, the way he looked at each of them that he wouldn't hesitate to make them a distant memory without hesitation. His body and demeanor was as much a weapon as anything that could be put in his large hands.

"Elliot." Bernard stood. "Come on in."

Elliot closed the door behind him and came fully into the room. His expression was unreadable as he approached the trio.

"Elliot Morgan, Jean Wallington and Ashley Temple."

Jean extended her hand, which he shook. "Ashley is one of our most skilled Cartel members," she said.

He turned slightly to his right. His jaw clenched. He extended his hand. "Pleasure," he murmured taking her hand.

Ashley offered a tight-lipped smile and a short nod of her head.

Elliot pulled up an available seat.

"We were briefing Ashley on the situation and the plan that we've designed. I want you both to know that we understand perfectly that this assignment is out of the norm for you. I know you had your reservations, Elliot about working with someone."

"It's not what I do," he said tersely. He turned to Ashley. "No offense, but I work alone." His hard gaze dared her to refute him.

Ashley lifted her chin. "I feel the same way," she tossed back ready to go toe-to-toe.

"But as you both know," Jean cut in, "in this business it's what's best for the operation and not our personal preferences." Her stern green gaze went from one tight face to the other.

"If we didn't think the two of you were the right ones for this assignment we could have easily gotten someone else," Bernard firmly stated. "Your expertise with uncovering information and taking on whatever persona necessary is going to be an asset," he said to Elliot. Then he turned to Ashley. "You have an excellent record of getting suspects to trust you. That was apparent on your last assignment. Those are some of the skills we need," he added, addressing them both.

"And we needed two operatives who didn't have any personal attachments that would hamper the assignments," Jean said.

"You mean, 'Who didn't have a life,' " Elliot said, his tone sarcastic as he tossed a meaningful look at Ashley.

Her eyes flashed. She pushed up from her seat. "Look, I'm sorry that you went to all of this trouble, but I'm not the one for this job." She snatched up her purse.

Bernard caught her wrist. "Wait. Please, sit down."

She drew in a long breath, cutting her eyes at Elliot before returning to her seat.

"Short temper is a hazard in the field," Elliot said in that low-key timbre, as he fingered the stud in his ear.

"Elliot," Bernard said, the one word more a warning than a salutation.

"I don't see how this is going to work," Ashley said, crossing her long legs. "It's clear that we won't be able to get along."

"You're going to have to find a way to work it out," Jean admonished. "This can't be about the two of you. This is about saving families from tragedy and young children from a life of misery or worse. So put your personal differences aside and keep your eyes on the prize — finding out who is behind the black-market baby operation in New York City. Are we clear?"

Silence enveloped the room.

"Well?"

"Fine," Elliot conceded.

Ashley smiled inwardly over the fact that he caved first. "Of course."

"You're both professionals. You'll work it out," Bernard said. "You're going to have to, especially since you will not only be working together, but living together as well."

"What!" they yelled in harmony, simultaneously leaping up out of their seats. Their choreography was so perfect, if the situation weren't so absurd it would be funny. They glared at each other.

"Sit down!" Jean slapped her palm against the desk. She snatched her glasses off and pinned them both with a withering gaze. "Enough. If the two of you thought this was some sort of democracy, you're wrong. It's not. You are a federal agent, Mr. Morgan. You don't get to pick and choose. Ashley on the other hand is not." She looked at Ashley. "So if you think you can't *handle* this assignment, leave now."

Ashley was so furious that her insides shook. He was an arrogant bastard! And it was clear from everything he'd said and the way he'd addressed her that he didn't think much of her or her abilities. How in the world were they going to live under the same roof? But she wouldn't let him get the best of her. And she certainly didn't want Jean to think that she couldn't handle the likes of Elliot Morgan. If she did, it would compromise anything she was assigned in the future.

"Two separate bedrooms," Ashley demanded more than stated.

"Fine with me," Elliot said, a twinkle in his dark eyes.

"Of course," Jean said. "Now, can we get back to the business at hand without any more outbursts?"

Ashley and Elliot settled back in their seats and listened to the plan.

More than an hour later the meeting ended. Ashley and Elliot each had a folder of information that they had to commit to memory, because once they opened the envelope the contents would evaporate from the page after more than an hour in the open air. It detailed their cover — who they were pretending to be until the case was solved — and several possible scenarios to gain access to the list of fertility clinics and adoption centers around the city.

Before they left they were told to stop in and see Jasmine, The Cartel's techno whiz. She would provide them with their new identification, and the dummy bank account they would share. Jean was making arrangements for the apartment that they would move into within the week. Everything was falling into step except Elliot and Ashley.

"After you," Elliot said as they left Jasmine's office.

Ashley looked up at him and caught the half grin on his lips. She brushed passed him. "Don't play the gentleman for my benefit," she snapped.

"Still testy," he murmured as he followed her up the stairs to the first-floor exit.

She stopped in her tracks and spun around nearly colliding into his hard-muscled chest. The heady scent of his cologne clouded her thoughts. For a moment she forgot her retort then her good sense returned. "Look, the less we have to say to each other the better. Just do your job and I'll do mine. How's that?" She didn't wait for a response but turned and strutted out leaving the door swinging on its hinges.

Elliot stepped outside and watched her as she walked down the street with her head high, looking neither left nor right. He leaned against the fence, took out his pack of cigarettes and stuck one in his mouth. He lit the tip and watched a curl of smoke float into the air. He'd been in enemy territory before. Ashley Temple would be a walk in the park. He strode off in the opposite direction.

Ashley gripped the steering wheel so hard her palms began to sting. She couldn't get the smug image of Elliot Morgan out of her head. The way he looked at her. The way he moved. The way he . . . smelled. Her heart thudded and she frowned in annoyance.

But if she was honest with herself, it was more than Elliot that had her mind spinning. It was the assignment: missing children. Did Jean know the truth? The nightmare was still as fresh in her spirit today as it was more than two decades ago. Her throat clenched as those horrible days bloomed anew.

CHAPTER 3

Ashley found a parking space a block away from the office. She took the time walking to compose herself before Mia read the anxiety all over her face. Living with a man she didn't know! Even for The Cartel that was asking a bit much. What made them think that she and Mr. Arrogance could ever in this lifetime work together?

She was going to have to do some serious meditating in order to ready herself for the assignment. Even if it was the highest of compliments to be chosen by Jean for two assignments in a row, she wasn't sure that she was cut out for this one.

Ashley pushed open the door to MT Management, Mia Turner's event-planning business and was pleased to see Savannah and her baby daughter, Mikayla.

"Hey! This is a surprise." Ashley dropped her purse on one of the desks and went straight to Mikayla and scooped her up for a kiss. "How's my girl? Look at you, looking all beautiful." She nuzzled her neck to squeals of delight.

"Can't a sister get some love?" Savannah asked in mock hurt.

Ashley waved her hand in dismissal. "Later." She went on kissing and hugging the baby before finally setting her back down in the stroller. "What brings you here? Off today?" She kissed Savannah's cheek.

"Took an R&R day. My boss was working me to the bone." She laughed good-naturedly. "Plus I needed to spend some time with my pumpkin," she added, stroking her daughter's curly head. "Thought we could do lunch. Danielle is on her way."

"Sounds like a plan."

"I hear you got another assignment."

"Word travels fast in this town." She plopped down into the seat opposite Savannah and stretched her legs out in front of her.

Savannah giggled. "What's a little espionage between friends."

"Yeah," she said halfheartedly.

Savannah tilted her head to the side. "Problem?"

Ashley blew out a breath of frustration. "Something like that."

"Hey, Ash," Mia said breezing into the

waiting area from her back office. "How'd it go with Jean?"

"Since we're doing lunch today, why don't I wait until we're all together."

As if on cue, Danielle came sailing in, fashionable as always and dramatically swept off her sunglasses. "Hey all." She looked from one face to another. "Gee, I feel like I walked into an intervention. What's up?"

"Ashley said she'd tell us over lunch," Mia offered.

Danielle arched a brow. "Sounds serious."

"Not that bad, but bad enough," Ashley said.

"So why are we all sitting around," Danielle said. "I want to hear this."

The stunning quartet gathered purses, keys, cell phones and stroller and headed out.

They arrived at their favorite eatery, The Shop. They'd been coming as a group for so long, they had their own booth and the waitstaff knew them by name.

The quartet settled down in their seats and flipped open their menus.

"Does this little gathering call for drinks?" Danielle asked.

"I could sure use one," Ashley said. "But

it's still early. Oh, what the heck. Let's order a round."

"That serious, huh?" Savannah asked.

Ashley sighed and leaned back against the worn brown leather seat. "I'm probably making more out of this than necessary, but the whole thing just rubs me the wrong way."

Phyllis, the waitress, came to take their orders. It was a round of their favorite, grilled salmon salad with tahini dressing and mojitos. With that out of the way, all eyes were on Ashley.

She told them about her meeting with Jean and Bernard.

"So far so good," Mia said.

"Then in walks Elliot Morgan."

Three pairs of eyes widened as Ashley described their meeting and the not-very-subtle animosity that flashed between them.

"He's pompous, arrogant and so full of himself," Ashley groaned. "And they want us to live together!" She folded her arms and pouted like a three-year-old.

The women broke out into laughter.

"Girl, your problem is you haven't had a man in your air space in so long you don't know how to handle it." Savannah chuckled.

"For real," Danielle concurred.

Ashley was visibly appalled at the lack of

support from her girls. They were supposed to be on her side. Sure, she hadn't had a real relationship in longer than she cared to admit. She knew she had commitment issues, deep-seated fears of loss. Loss that she hadn't shared with anyone, not even her girls. There was a part of her that believed she didn't deserve someone to care about her and her about them. The guilt of all those years ago still haunted her.

They all nodded, biting back smirks. Even little Mikayla was laughing and kicking her feet in her stroller.

Mia leaned forward, schooling her expression. "Look, sis, no one knows better than me how weird it can be living with a man. When Steven and I got together it was tough at first."

"Yeah, but he's your *man*. Now your husband. That's something completely different. I don't know this jerk from a hole in the wall."

"You did say he looked like Idris Elba, didn't you?" Danielle said, egging her on.

Ashley rolled her eyes.

"Look, it's just an assignment. You'll have separate rooms and separate lives outside of the case," Savannah said, always the practical one. "Just worry about the job."

That was just it, Ashley thought. The job.

But maybe Savannah was right. Focus on the assignment. It may well lead her to what she'd been searching for over the past twenty years — answers.

Elliot turned the key in the door of his third-floor walk-up on West Eighth Street in the Village. He'd found the place after a less-than-exhaustive search, but fell for it right away. His apartment was in a prewar building, with vaulted ceilings and enormous rooms. His one-bedroom apartment in any other neighborhood in Manhattan would go for three times the amount with the rooms cut down to bite-sized pieces. The neighborhood was an eclectic blend of class, culture, language and age, from seedy to high end and everything in between. It was a mecca for the artsy and a paradise for lovers of music, avante-garde shops and cozy cafès. The perfect place to blend in, able to see and go unseen.

He locked the door behind him and began tugging his fitted T-shirt over his head as he strolled from the front hallway, through the mostly unfurnished living room to his bedroom located in the back, facing the park. He tossed his shirt on the bed and absently rubbed the raised, circular scar on his shoulder, the result of a gunshot wound from a man who wished he'd been a better shot. Elliot clenched his teeth. He'd been distracted that afternoon in the alley, by memories of the argument he'd had with Lynn the night before.

It's the first rule in his line of work; relationships are a distraction. Hit It and Quit It, was the slogan among the guys. He should have listened. Then what happened later would not have mattered as much, wouldn't have hurt him so much. It changed him. Now he was a poster child for the boy's club mantra.

Elliot pulled the envelope he'd gotten from Jean out of his back pocket. He unfolded it and tried to flatten it out on the bed by running his fist over it. It refused to succumb to his manipulations and curled back up.

"Figures," he groused, flopping spread-eagle across the bed. He tossed a thick, muscled arm across his eyes and a crystal clear image of Ashley popped behind his lids with such preciseness, the near-reality shot a jolt of denied longing to his groin. He felt his shaft throb and jump against the zipper of his jeans. "Down boy," he grumbled, and forced his mind to the issue at hand — a new, unwanted assignment. He was a field operative. His specialty search and dispose. As a former Navy Seal he'd been trained for combat, for dealing swiftly and with stealth against the unseen enemy before he joined the FBI and worked as a part-time handyman for the CIA in their even shadier operations. This assignment was a slap in the face. Missing babies! He didn't even like kids. They were a nuisance. Not to mention messy and noisy.

He ran through a laundry list of higher-ups that he may have pissed off to get saddled with this assignment and couldn't come up with anyone. He lurched forward and sat up, snatched the envelope and opened it.

It pretty much laid out what Jean and Bernard explained earlier. But in reading the documents, he got a sudden chill when he went over some of the pain-filled stories of the parents whose infants went missing. Included in the envelope was a list of adoption centers, fertility clinics and local hospitals.

A deep frown creased his brow. What kind of person would steal a baby from its parents? But he knew the answer. Money and greed were great motivators, and combined with persons of no conscience made for ugly scenarios. He released a heavy sigh as the ink began to fade on the pages.

These parents deserved some justice, he concluded. So he'd just suck it up and bring a clean and quick end to this madness. A half grin lifted the side of his full mouth. As a minor benefit he'd get to play hubby with the very sexy Ashley Temple, whether she liked it or not. He chuckled at the thought.

CHAPTER 4

"So are you feeling a little better about things?" Mia asked once she and Ashley had returned to the office.

Ashley gave a slight shrug of her shoulder. "I suppose." She turned to Mia, her hand planted on her slender hips. "I've never lived with a man. Let alone a perfect stranger." She frowned. "I like my independence."

Mia dropped her oversized purse on the desk and looked at her friend. "Is that all that's *really* bothering you?"

Ashley glanced away for an instant then looked at Mia. She almost smiled. "He is kinda fine in a pain-in-the-ass sort of way."

They both giggled.

Ashley dropped her tense shoulders. "I guess it will be all right. The main thing is finding out who is behind the stealing and selling of babies." A shiver ran through her.

"Exactly."

Ashley pushed a smile onto her face,

highlighting her prominent cheekbones. "So," she said on a breath, "what's on the agenda for today?"

But even as Mia ran down the list of upcoming events they had to take care of, Ashley's mind was elsewhere. *Elliot Morgan. Babies. Twenty years. Maybe this is a blessing in disguise.*

Ashley walked through her small one-bedroom apartment, which she'd worked diligently on to transform from the drab place she'd originally rented into her cozy abode. Being an R&B music buff, she had one wall in her living room dedicated to some of her favorite artists: Smokey Robinson, Stevie, Luther, Gladys, Anita Baker, The Temps, James Brown, Michael Jackson, Jazmine Sullivan, Earth, Wind & Fire, Frankie Beverly and Maze, and Maxwell to name a few. Her collection was extensive, going back to some classic 45s and collector's items album covers.

The sparkling wood floors were dotted with oversized pillows, low tables and standing plants. Rather than curtains or blinds in the windows, they were covered with hanging philodendrons.

But her bedroom was truly her sanctuary. Her queen-sized bed with its downy pillow-top mattress took up much of the small space. But it was truly fit for a queen. To conserve room, she had her flat screen television mounted on the wall. The one great amenity was the walk-in closet that housed her extensive wardrobe, another one of her addictions — clothes.

That brought to mind these new living arrangements. How was she going to get along without her music and all of her clothes and shoes? Sighing she tugged off her cropped sweater and put it in the bag for the cleaner.

She sat down on the foot of the bed and pulled off her ankle boots, just as her cell phone began to ring. She pulled it from the case on her hip and frowned at the unfamiliar number. She pressed the talk icon.

"Hello?"

"Hi. Ashley?"

The low timbre shimmied up her spine. "Who is this?"

"Sorry. It's E — uh, Elliot Morgan."

Her heart bumped against her chest. She cleared her throat. "Oh," was all she could sputter as she tried to get her brain to catch up with the fact that he was on the phone.

"Look, I know I was being a jerk earlier today. And we, uh, probably got off on the wrong foot."

Her brows rose in surprise. "Probably,"

she teased and could almost see a smile on his face. She crossed her legs.

"So I was thinking that before we do this live-in thing maybe we should try to get to know each other . . . first."

"Meaning?"

"Have you had dinner?"

"No, I haven't." She swallowed over the sudden knot in her throat.

"Can I interest you in dinner?"

What the hell! Was he asking her out on a date? Her pulsed pounded and her thoughts short-circuited.

"Hey, maybe that was a bad idea. Guess I'll see you on moving —"

"No. I'm sorry. You just caught me off guard. Dinner. Sure."

"I can pick you up in about an hour. Is that enough time?"

Her eyes widened even further. A real date. "Okay." She started to give him her address.

"I already have it. In the file," he added by way of explanation.

"If Jean is nothing else, she's thorough. I'll see you in an hour."

"Right." He hung up.

Ashley sat with the phone in her hand for a good two minutes mesmerized by what had transpired. Maybe the "real" Elliot

Morgan would show up at dinner. She shook her head, her spiral curls and twists dancing on her head. Taking a quick look at her watch, she hopped up from her bed and began peeling off her clothes as she darted for the shower.

After numerous wardrobe changes, she'd finally settled on elegantly casual. She selected a pair of black straight-legged jeans, a pearl-gray blouse that shimmered in the right light, with a black silk button-up sweater. She was only five foot six in bare feet and Elliot was well over six foot, so she opted for her Ferragamo black ankle boots that oozed comfort even after long hours on your feet. She captured her hair carefree away from her face with a sparkling gray head band, pulling it into a halo around her face. Minimal makeup, a dab of African musk behind her ears and on her wrists and she was ready just as the doorbell rang.

Her stomach wobbled for a second and heat popped in her ears. She took a quick look in the mirror, left her bedroom and scanned the living room en route to the door, confident that everything was in its place. She went to the intercom, confirmed that it was Elliot and buzzed him in. Her heart pounded. Moments later her front doorbell rang. Straightening, she grasped the knob, turned it and opened the door.

The air stopped in her lungs. She wasn't sure what to expect, but seeing him again did something to her that she couldn't explain if you paid her. Everything about him was more intense, more magnified, bigger and brighter than when she'd seen him for the first time.

Was it the dark, searing eyes that seemed to peek into her soul from beneath half-lowered lids and silky lashes, or the cool chocolate of his complexion that blended seamlessly with his shirt, slacks and hip-length suede jacket? The combination so enticing and perfectly matched that his attire was more second skin than a cover-up. Perhaps it was the half smile that moved like a lazy river across his full lips giving just a hint of beautiful teeth.

"Hey," he said, his low, almost gritty voice snapping her out of her momentary trance.

"Hi. Come on in. I need to get my jacket and purse." She turned and commanded her lungs to inhale and exhale as she crossed the space on shaky legs, knew he was watching the sway of her hips and prayed that not only did he like what he saw, but that she didn't trip.

Miraculously she made it to her bedroom.

She drew in long, calming breaths of air. Blinking several times she focused on what she needed to do. She took her purse from the top of her dresser, checked for her cell phone, ID, house keys and wallet. She took her jacket from the back of the overstuffed armchair that sat like a Buddha near her window then went back out front.

She entered the room and watched him for an instant. He was turned halfway away from her, running his finger along the frame of a photograph that rested on a table in the short hall. His body was fluid almost as if it moved to some sultry beat in his head, so different from the tightly coiled man of earlier in the day. "All ready," she announced.

He only turned his head in her direction, let his eyes run over her for a hot flash of an instant. "Cool. Let's go."

Elliot opened the door for her and as she passed him she caught the faintest hint of something manly, a clean and seductive scent that was more him than off the shelf. She liked it. She locked the door behind them.

"Did you have someplace in mind?" she asked as they walked down the stairs to the outside door. She felt his heat as he walked inches from her on the wide staircase.

"Why don't I surprise you?"

She glanced up at him as he reached around her to open the door. His arm brushed her shoulder and she was certain she felt a jolt of heat race down to the pads of her fingers.

"I like surprises," she said. "Most of the time."

"We'll hope for the best."

They stepped outside into the cool spring night. He pointed to a midnight blue Jaguar parked across the street.

"You're getting paid too much, or I'm in the wrong business," she teased him as he opened the door of the lush automobile, its interior still carrying the scent of brand-new leather.

"Every now and then you have to treat yourself, especially in this business," he said, as they settled in the car. "Unfortunately, I'm out of the country so much I rarely get a chance to drive it."

Ashley fastened her seat belt. "How often do you . . . travel?"

He put the car in gear and she felt the gentle hum of the motor vibrate beneath her. Or was it more than the car that had her vibrating?

His jaw tightened. "I'm usually out of the country eight to ten months a year." A hardness settled over his face, sending his prominent features into sharp relief.

"Hey, I'm sorry," she said. "It's obvious that's not something you want to talk about."

He turned his head in her direction as he pulled up to a red light. For a moment he took in her profile, the slight jut of her chin, the long lashes that shadowed her eyes, the pert nose and firm set of her glossy lips. Everything about the way she stared straight ahead to the line of her shoulders indicated that he'd done it again — went on the attack for no good reason. At least none that anyone other than himself would understand. It was complicated, too complicated to explain the kind of limbo life that he lived. His constant sense of disconnection, waking up day after day not knowing where he was or who he was pretending to be.

"Sorry," he offered. "Tough topic. Let's talk about something else." He gripped the steering wheel a bit tighter as her intoxicating scent wafted beneath his nose.

"Have you ever lived with a woman before?" she boldly asked.

Elliot tossed his head back and laughed from the pit of his gut. "You're definitely direct," he said, still chuckling.

A tiny smile teased the corners of her

mouth. "So I've been told," she tossed back. She angled her gaze in his direction. "Well?"

He drew in a breath and relaxed against the smooth leather interior. "Actually, no. This will be a first for me." He turned to look at her and their gazes bumped against each other for what felt like a blissful eternity.

A car horn blared behind them. They both jerked away from the thing that held them in place. Elliot pressed down on the gas and took them across the intersection.

He cleared his throat. "So, uh, what about you?"

"No." She paused. "Guess it'll be the first time for the both of us."

His mind went racing off in a million directions at once, all of them forcing him to adjust his position in his seat. Was this the same uptight, headstrong woman he'd met earlier? He knew there was fire beneath her she-warrior armor, but this was the kind of fire that burned from the inside out. Then his years of dealing with adversaries and those pretending to be something that they weren't kicked in.

"The lounge is on the next block," he said, changing subjects to one in which he could control. "Hopefully I can find a parking space."

Ashley instantly noticed the shift in attitude and the sudden cool breeze in the car. She flicked a brow in dismissal and folded her arms. *Just like I said in the beginning,* she mused to herself, *a pain in the ass.* This was going to be a long night.

CHAPTER 5

They spent the next few minutes of the drive in an unspoken truce of silence. Ashley zeroed in on the passing traffic and pedestrians as if they were creations of the great Da Vinci and she had been commissioned to unlock the mysteries of the swaths of color and movement. In reality she didn't see a thing, blinded by flashes of red as her temper continued to boil. Her body curled into a tighter and tighter knot of tension as the minutes ticktocked in her head.

Why was it so easy for him to irritate her to the point of distraction? She'd had her share of relationships. She knew how to handle men — both casual and serious. Elliot Morgan was a new breed, however. Her lips tightened into a line so thin as to be almost invisible.

She was so intent on her ire that she didn't realize they'd come to a stop until her door was pulled open and Elliot's large hand was extended for her to take. She blinked and looked up into his face. Whatever it was that had her coiled tight enough to snap, slowly began to unwind, and she felt the slow thud of her heart against her chest. The veil of red that had descended in front of her eyes was lifted, and even in the twilight of evening she could see sunshine.

She made herself breathe as she placed her hand in his and felt the strength of his grasp pull her to her feet. He didn't bother to step back. When she stood there was a mere breath that separated them. For a moment they faced each other and she sank into the depth of his dark eyes and traveled to exotic places along the planes of his face.

"It's right up the street," he said, his voice low, stroking her below her waist as surely as if he actually touched her there.

She bobbed her head and muttered, "Okay."

He moved back to give her room and she felt as if a chasm had opened in front of her and she longed for the security of his warmth and closeness. Somehow he managed to reach around her to close the car door, having her momentarily encircled in his warmth. He gave her a half smile and extended his hand in the direction of the club. Ashley fell in step beside him doubling her pace to keep up with his long stride.

The half-block-long line signaled that they had arrived.

"Wow, it must be packed," Ashley said. "We'll never get in." She peered around the line of bodies.

"Not a problem." He took her hand and walked her past the crowd, right up to the front door. "Hey, Lou," he greeted the muscled man at the door. When Lou's tight gaze and even tighter expression landed on Elliot, he actually smiled.

"Oh, man! Good to see you, brother. You have a lovely guest, I see." He stepped aside to let them pass.

Ashley smiled.

"Be sure to see Gina," Lou continued. "She'll hook you up with some good seats."

Elliot clapped Lou on the back. "Thanks, man."

"For you . . . anytime. Don't be a stranger."

Elliot had yet to let go of Ashley's hand, and the longer he held it the more she liked it.

"I take it you've been here before," she teased.

Elliot chuckled. "Yeah, the owners are friends of mine. Nick Hunter and Sam Blackstone. If they're around I'll be sure to introduce you . . . in case you and your friends want to stop by sometime." He guided her to the hostess podium. "Gina," he cooed at the modelesque woman, who was at least six feet tall with sharp Ethiopian features — voluminous dark eyes, sweeping forehead and high cheekbones. Her long, slender neck gave her an even more regal appearance. Her ruby-red lips spread into a slow smile as her long lashes lowered over her eyes. She leaned forward taking Elliot's face in her hands and kissing each cheek.

"You bad boy," she scolded. "Where have you been? It's been much too long." Her accent was unrecognizable, a combination of nations that melded into something unique.

Elliot chuckled from deep in his chest. He looked deep into her eyes, lowered his voice. "Now, Gina, you know if I told you, I'd have to make you disappear."

Gina tossed her head back on her long stem of a neck and laughed an almost musical melody. "You and your secret games." She finally turned her attention to Ashley. "Welcome to Rhythms. Do not let this man charm you into doing anything naughty. He can be very persuasive."

"I'll keep that in mind," Ashley said, not sure if the quickening in her stomach was from being let in on some private joke or the fact that Gina may have been a willing recipient of Elliot's charms.

"I'll show you to your table." She took two menus from the stand and led them to the center of the club with a table in front of the stage.

Elliot helped Ashley into her seat.

"Nick is playing tonight," Gina said, placing the menus in front of them. "You're in luck. Maybe you can sit in on a set."

Elliot chuckled and shook his head. "I'm too rusty to get up there with the boys. It's been a while." He leaned casually back in his chair, his thighs spread and his arm draped across the top of the seat.

"Your server will be along to get your drink order." She focused on Ashley. "You should convince him to play tonight." Gina squeezed his shoulder and gave him a quick wink before walking away.

Elliot lowered his head for a moment and shook it as he chuckled softly.

Ashley rested her forearms on the table and leaned forward. "So what is it that I should be convincing you to play?"

"Naw. Don't even go there." He waved off her question and almost looked embarrassed, his usual swagger momentarily gone.

"Why? Got something to hide?"

His gaze connected with hers. "No."

"Do you play some kind of weird instrument?"

"No."

"Tuba?"

"No," he sputtered.

"Harp?"

"Very funny."

"Banjo!"

He cracked a smile.

"I got it. The recorder!" Her eyes widened in delight.

Elliot laughed. "Not since I was about six," he confessed.

"I knew it," she teased and sat back, waiting expectantly.

"Trumpet," he finally admitted.

She tipped her head to the side in appreciation. "Really? Wow. That's Miles Davis's instrument of choice."

"So you know a little something about music. I should have figured as much with that collection you have at your place."

She grinned. "One of my passions." She paused. "So, how long has it been since you've played?"

He thought about the last time he performed. It was before his last assignment in Europe, which lasted nearly ten months, before everything got so dark and ugly and he couldn't tell the good guys from the bad, right from wrong. He glanced away. "A while," he said, his voice distant and detached, almost wistful, Ashley thought.

She watched his profile in the light and shadows of the club and the parade of emotions that loosened and tightened his jaw. "I hear it's like bike riding. You never forget, you just have to get back on."

He ran his tongue across his lips. His eyes settled on her mouth for a moment and Ashley felt a sudden pulse beat between her legs. She adjusted herself in the seat.

"That's what you heard, huh? Just get back on?" His gaze bore into hers.

A warm flush rose up from the pit of her stomach and settled in the center of her chest. She drew in a breath. Her taunting challenges of only moments ago, having dissipated under his smoldering gaze and innuendo.

The waitress appeared to take their drink orders and the momentary spell was broken.

Elliot lifted his chin toward Ashley. "What would you like?"

You! Her body shouted, even as her mind remained in disagreement. *I want to find out if everything is as hard as those biceps and thighs.* She cleared her throat. "Hmm, apple martini, please. Frozen."

The waitress nodded. "And you, sir?"

"Courvoisier on the rocks."

"I'll be right back with your drinks."

The momentary reprieve gave Ashley the opportunity to pull herself together, take her eyes, mind and body off of Elliot and take in the surroundings.

The club gave off a feeling of back-in-the-day night spots of Harlem, dark, cozy, low music playing in the background, the smell of food wafting in the air.

"This place seems really nice," she said. "I don't know how I missed it."

"Nick had been negotiating to get it opened for a while. The building was abandoned and in pretty bad shape from what he told me. And not in the choicest of neighborhoods at the time."

"The neighborhood has definitely changed. There was a time when most folks wouldn't come over here at night."

Elliot nodded his agreement. "It's like that all over the city, Harlem in particular."

The waitress returned with their drinks and set them on the table. "Are you ready to order or do you need a few minutes?" She looked from one to the other.

"Any suggestions?" Ashley asked.

"The seared salmon is excellent," she said. "Or if you prefer we have stuffed chicken breast, hot wings, crab cakes, salads . . ."

Ashley turned her attention to Elliot and lifted her brows in question.

"You can't go wrong with the crab cakes," he said.

Ashley nodded with a smile. "I'll have the crab cakes and wild rice with a small side salad."

"Make that two," Elliot said.

"Great." She collected the menus and walked off.

Just as they turned their attention toward each other, the contact was broken once again.

"E!"

A tall, dark and extremely handsome man came up and clapped Elliot on the back. Elliot looked up and his expression beamed with pleasure. He pushed back from his seat and stood and the two Adonises — one more gorgeous than the other — did that hearty man-hug thing.

"Wow, my brother, when did you get back in town and why didn't you call me?"

Elliot chuckled deep in his gut. "Look, man I just got back day before yesterday. Getting my legs back under me."

"Yeah, yeah," he teased, throwing his arm around Elliot's broad shoulder, and turned to Ashley. "And who is this beautiful lady?"

Elliot extended his hand toward Ashley. "Ashley Temple, this is Nick Hunter, the coowner of this joint."

Nick cut him a look, then shot Ashley with a smile that could melt a glacier. "My pleasure." He came around to Ashley's side of the table and shook her hand. "Welcome to Rhythms."

"Thank you. You have a great place."

Nick straightened and tugged in a deep breath. "It took some work," he said with obvious pleasure, "but we did it." He turned back to Elliot. "You guys have everything you need?"

"Yeah, yeah," Elliot said.

"Tonight is on the house. A welcome-back gift," he said to Elliot, "and a welcome, too," he said to Ashley. He started backing up. "Gotta get ready for my set. You know you're playing tonight so get your lips together."

"Man, come on," Elliot said.

"Forget it. Not taking no for an answer." He walked off, grinning.

Elliot flopped back against the cushion of the chair. Ashley giggled.

"The only way out is to leave now. And I have no intention on missing out on those crab cakes." She folded her arms beneath her breasts and challenged him with her steady gaze.

A slow smile crept across his mouth. "Must be some kind of conspiracy," he groused good-naturedly, hiding his soul by lowering his lids over his dark eyes.

"How long have you been playing trumpet?"

"Since high school. Played in the school band."

"You!" she said, delight shining in her eyes and lifting her voice.

He chuckled. "Yeah, go figure. My folks thought it would keep me out of trouble."

"Did it?"

He shrugged. "Not according to them."

"I can imagine you must have been a handful."

His voice lowered, his eyes lifted and settled on her face. "Can you?"

Something hot and sweet moved around in the center of her chest. Slowly she ran her tongue across her mouth, tried to swallow and couldn't. She reached for her drink and took a short sip.

"Well?"

Her brows rose. "Well, what?"

"You said you can imagine me being a handful. I asked you if you could."

"Oh —" she glanced at the table "— You give the impression that you would do all the things that little boys do."

He eased closer across the table. "And what do you imagine us little boys doing?"

Her eyes crinkled with laughter. "Chasing dogs, tugging little girls' ponytails."

He slowly spun his glass on the table. "When little boys grow up they stop tugging ponytails and chasing puppies. They'd rather —"

Before he could finish, their food arrived and the lights dimmed on the stage as the band took their places.

"Welcome to Rhythms!" Nick said, taking the microphone. The room erupted into applause. "We have a full night of entertainment for you, and I want you to put your hands together for my man Elliot Morgan who will be joining us tonight on trumpet."

Ashley applauded with all the others, her hands clapping high above her head. "Whoo-hooo," she shouted, laughing heartily.

He wagged a warning finger at her that only made her laugh harder.

The band began with an original composition then segued to several standards, which all had the rapt audience bobbing their head and popping their fingers. From her perfect position at the table, Ashley could watch Elliot's every move, catch every nuance and expression. What she saw was a man who was comfortable in his own skin, who could easily transition from gentleman to lethal weapon in the blink of an eye, thoughtful, funny, talented and heartbreakingly sexy all rolled up into one fine package. It could be so easy for her to succumb to his obvious charms, but the reality was they were partners in the investigation of a serious crime. Taking it beyond business was inappropriate, not to mention that he simply rubbed her the wrong way.

Her musings were interrupted when Nick took the mic and announced to the crowd that Elliot would be joining them for the rest of their set. Whoops and hollers of approval, along with the house spotlight followed Elliot's reluctant progression from his seat to his place on the stage, where Sammy handed him his instrument of choice. "We've been keeping it warm for ya," Sammy whispered, as Elliot removed his trumpet from the case.

For a moment he looked at it with a mixture of awe and reverence. He'd left it in Nick's care when he took off months ago for Europe. A smile moved slowly across his mouth as the gold valves glistened against the muted light almost like a beacon.

Elliot lifted the trumpet out of the case,

reached for a reed and fixed it to the lip of the instrument. Slowly he brought it to his mouth, shut his eyes and blew out several notes to test the quality, range and his rusty skills. Satisfied, he turned to Nick and gave him a short nod of his head.

Nick eased into Miles Davis's "The Man with the Horn," and Elliot picked up on the melody as if he'd never been away from his trumpet.

Ashley was mesmerized by this *new* Elliot that was on the stage. He was a chameleon, ever changing. The moment she thought she had him pegged, he'd switch up on her, leaving her to question her instincts.

He finished out the set with the band to jubilant applause before hopping down off stage and returning to his table. Ashley was still applauding, a smile beaming across her face.

"You were fantastic!" she enthused, grabbing his hand before she could stop herself.

The spontaneous moment stunned them both. Elliot's gaze fell to the hand that covered his. Embarrassed, she pulled her hand away but not before Elliot caught it. He looked into her eyes as his fingers grazed hers.

"So you liked it?" he said, his voice low and intimate. He ran his thumb across her knuckles.

Ashley's pulse throbbed. "I don't know why you doubted yourself," she managed to say. "You were right at home up there."

"Didn't want to make a total fool of myself," he half joked, "especially with you watching."

"Can I get you anything else from the bar?" the waitress said, snapping the line of tension between them. She picked up the empty plates and looked from one to the other.

Ashley took the reprieve to ease her hand out of Elliot's warm grasp. "I'm fine, thanks."

Elliot lifted his half-empty glass. "I'll have another."

"Right away."

Elliot leaned back in his chair and appraised Ashley from beneath lowered lashes.

"What?" she finally said, after his stare began to make her uncomfortable.

He gave a slow, short shake of his head. "Can't quite figure you out."

"What's that supposed to mean?"

"Don't get twisted out of shape. I'm just saying I can't figure you out."

"Funny, I thought the same thing about you."

The corner of his mouth jerked up into a

grin. "Really?"

"It wasn't a compliment," she lightly teased.

He leaned forward. "It's late. I should get you home."

His sudden change in demeanor caught her off guard. Barely seconds ago he was practically in her lap and now he was ready to dismiss her like the final class of the day. She flicked a brow, and picked up her purse from the table.

"Ready when you are." She stood.

Elliot got up and took her jacket from the back of her chair. "I don't think so," he whispered and helped her put it on.

Ashley glanced at him over her shoulder, but his expression was unreadable. She adjusted her jacket and tucked her purse under her arm. The warmth of his hand at the small of her back seeped through the fabric. She walked just far enough ahead of him that he had no choice but to let go. For a moment she was smugly satisfied. She knew it was a childish little triumph, but she didn't care. How dare he turn off and on like a light and expect her to do the same? Who did he think he was anyway?

She pushed through the door and out into the cool evening. With every step they took in the direction of the car, she grew more annoyed. She stopped in mid-step and swung toward him just as his arm snaked around her waist and pulled her flush up against him. His dark eyes burned into hers and she could feel her heart banging against her chest.

"I'm not the one to play with," he said, barely moving his lips.

Her eyes widened in a mixture of alarm and sexual excitement. She could feel the hard lines of his body, the heat that rose from his skin, the danger that radiated from his eyes.

"I would give you the same warning," she said on a husky breath, "but I know you don't take advice very well." She pulled away from him and challenged him with a hard gaze of her own.

His mouth moved into a lazy grin and his soft chuckles taunted her. "Come on. I'm tired." He continued toward the car and she fell into silent step beside him.

Seething as she jammed the seat belt into place, she prayed for a quick end to this torturous assignment.

CHAPTER 6

Ashley awoke the following morning totally exhausted. For the few moments of sleep that she'd been able to catch, she'd been tormented by images of Elliot. He'd chased her throughout the night, turning up around corners, behind doors, at the end of every path she took. Each and every time he had that self-satisfied look on his face. But she'd always been able to slip out of his grasp. Just as he would reach out for her she would dart away. Until the last time. She'd struggled so hard to get out of his hold that she'd nearly fallen out of the bed.

So here she sat bone weary and bleary-eyed. At least it was Saturday and she didn't have to worry about going into the office. Groaning, she eased out of bed and shuffled to the bathroom for her morning rituals.

Feeling moderately better after a hot shower and pampering her skin in shea butter lotion, Ashley went to the kitchen to put on some coffee when the doorbell rang. Frowning, she tightened the belt on her robe and walked barefoot to her intercom.

"Who?"

"Ashley, it's me Bernard. Can I come up?"

Bernard! That was a twist. She buzzed him in. Moments later there was a light knock at the door.

"Is something wrong?" she asked as she stepped aside to let him in.

"No. I should have called first," he said, turning toward her. "It was kind of a spur-of-the-moment decision."

Slowly she shut the door then led the way to the living area. "Make yourself comfortable. I was making coffee. Want some?"

"Thanks. That would be great." He sat down on the edge of the love seat after taking off his jacket. He draped it across his lap.

Ashley stood in front of her coffee maker watching the hot liquid percolate and wondering what in the hell Bernard was doing sitting in her living room at ten on a Saturday morning. She took mugs from the cabinet and filled them to just below the rim. She brought his mug and set it down on the coffee table. "I only have soy milk and Sweet'n Low."

He waved away the offer. "Black is fine." She nodded and returned to the kitchen to finish fixing her coffee. Bernard was just getting off his cell phone when she took a seat opposite him on the couch. "So . . . what's up?" She took a sip from her mug and waited.

"I know that you as well as all the other Cartel members are used to working alone or at the very least, working with each other —"

"Listen, if you came all the way over here to lay down the law —"

He held up his hand. "Whoa, whoa, hear me out."

She drew in a breath and slowly let it go. "Sorry," she muttered.

"As I was saying, I know this goes against protocol. And I know that you and Elliot didn't hit it off . . ."

The mere mention of Elliot's name set off all of her bells and whistles. Coffee sloshed over the top of her mug and dribbled onto her lap. She grabbed a napkin from the table and dabbed at the spot, muttering under her breath.

". . . but Elliot is the best at what he does. He always has been. I know he can be rough around the edges. He's been through a great deal. Especially over the past two years."

Ashley sat up a bit straighter as she listened.

"Before he got sent out on his last assignment overseas, he'd lost his mother to cancer and months later, his younger brother to a drive-by. He internalizes. He blames himself."

"Why?" she dared to ask.

"He felt that he should have been there for his mother, found her the best doctor, the cure," he added throwing up his hands and shaking his head in frustration. "And his brother . . . he was always in trouble. He'd been trying to get his mother to move out of the neighborhood for years, but she'd refused." Bernard caught Ashley's focused gaze. "He nearly quit after the double whammy. It took more than a year for him to get back in the saddle. And this last year overseas was hard. Lives were lost. But the case was solved. I brought Elliot onto this case not only because he's good, but because he needs to decompress and wind down from a helluva rough two years."

Ashley swallowed the last of her coffee and slowly set down her cup. She didn't want to feel anything but animosity toward Elliot, but that silent pact she'd made with herself went out the window after listening to Bernard.

"He'd have a fit if he knew I said anything to you, but I thought that if you had a little insight into Elliot, it would help the two of you work together better to solve this case."

"I appreciate you telling me this. And I promise I'll never say a word to Elliot."

Bernard lowered his head and nodded then looked across at Ashley. "You two find the bastards that're stealing these kids." His jaw clenched as he pushed up from his seat. "Thanks for the coffee." He walked toward the door. With his hand on the knob he turned to Ashley. "You'll probably be hearing from Jean. She has the apartment and she'll want the two of you to take a look." He dug in his pocket and placed a gold band in her palm. "You'll be needing that."

She looked down and the gold sparkled back at her. Her heart thumped. "Thanks," she mumbled and closed the door behind him. *Wow, it wasn't even noon and her day was off to a flying start.* Her fingers closed around the ring and squeezed.

Of course, Ashley heard from Jean sooner rather than later and was informed that she was expected at the apartment at 3:00 p.m. and that she was *Mrs. Morgan.*

At five minutes to three, Ashley eased her Honda into an available parking spot on

West 121st Street, walking distance from the Cartel headquarters and the day spa, Pause for Men. She checked her BlackBerry for the address — 811. She turned off the car and stepped out, adjusting her purse on her shoulder. She verified the address then headed off toward her right. She stopped in front of a newly renovated, six-story apartment building and checked her watch. Three on the dot. A young woman came out of the front door carrying her Yorkie in her purse and hurried off down the street. Ashley sat down on one of the benches that braced either side of the glass-and-wood front door and waited.

Before she could get herself settled, she glanced down the street and saw Elliot and Jean coming her way. For some inexplicable reason the sight of Elliot caused a tingle of excitement to shimmy up the inside of her legs and settle into a fluttering pool in her center. Slowly she stood.

"Sorry if we kept you waiting," Jean said by way of a greeting, but offered no further explanation as she breezed by her. She took a key from her purse and opened the front door.

"Rest well?" Elliot said for only Ashley's ears as he held the door open for her.

She glanced quickly over her shoulder and

her gaze landed on the pulsing cords of his neck then slowly rose up to his lips that were set in a mocking grin. She almost rolled her eyes but didn't bother. "Fine," she said and caught up with Jean who stood in front of the elevator.

"The apartment is on the forth floor. Although the building is six stories, there are only six apartments. Each of them take up the entire floor from front to back. Plenty of room. No reason for either of you to get in the other's way."

Neither Elliot nor Ashley missed the barb.

The elevator doors slid open and the trio stepped in. Like sentinels they took up positions on either side of Jean and stared straight ahead. The door slid open on the fourth floor and Jean led them down the hallway to the front door.

"I'm sure you'll both be very comfortable," she said opening the door and stepping aside.

The loftlike apartment was straight out of *Architectural Digest* — low glass-and-chrome tables, russet leather furnishings drew the eye to the center space. Beyond wooden arches was the dining room with a table that easily sat six. The open entryway veered left and right, set on gleaming hardwood floors with rafters to match in a deep, chocolate brown with a hint of red. Light beamed in from insanely high windows.

"There are bedrooms on either side, with a private bath in each. The kitchen is around this corner." Jean led the way to a state-of-the-art, stainless-steel heaven for even the most reluctant cook. The island in the center of the kitchen had four jets, a sink and built-in wok. The oven and double-door fridge stood on either side of the deep sink. Counters and cabinets of the same rich wood as the front room ran around the perimeter of the kitchen. "The cabinets and fridge are fully stocked. We tried to anticipate your needs. There's also a laundry room for your use." Jean pulled open a door that exposed a room nearly the size of a small bedroom that housed a washer and dryer, shelving and racks to hang clothes. Jean swept out of the room and returned to the front. She reached inside her purse, pulled out a thick folder and dropped it on the kitchen counter. "I suggest you stop by your respective apartments, pick up your essentials then get settled down to married life and this case," she said, lifting her chin toward the folder. "I'll be in touch." Jean moved toward the front door and walked out.

"I get to keep the crib in the divorce

settlement," Elliot teased.

Ashley turned toward him and couldn't fight back the smile moving across her mouth. "Don't make me do a Madea on you and saw everything in half," Ashley tossed back referring to Tyler Perry's *Diary of a Mad Black Woman.*

Elliot tossed his head back and laughed, a deep soul-stirring laugh that warmed Ashley from the inside out, and for a hot minute she imagined what it would be like to hear his robust laughter each day. "Oh, you are dangerous," he said, wagging a finger at her. "You want me to drop you by your place to pick your stuff up?"

"Thanks for the offer. But I have my car."

He nodded slowly, his dark gaze rolling over her. "The only place she didn't show us is the bedrooms."

Her heart knocked in her chest. She looked away from him and walked over to the fridge. She pulled open one of the double doors. "She was right, fully stocked." She took out an apple from a bowl on the bottom shelf. When she stood and closed the door, Elliot was right there. Her breath caught and stuck in her throat.

"Any more apples?" he said, but she would swear in a court of law that wasn't what he was really asking.

She swallowed and handed him hers. The hint of a grin lifted the corner of his mouth before he took a deep bite. She was mesmerized by the way his lips played with the fruit, the movement of his jaw as he chewed. She could almost taste the succulent juice that exploded in his mouth. Her nostrils flared and she tugged the door open to separate them, gave herself some room to breathe. She took another apple, slammed the door shut and walked out.

Elliot strolled out behind her his eyes glued on the sway of her hips encased in the form-fitting jeans. Well at least they had what could serve as a small football field to separate their respective bedrooms, he mused. Besides, Ashley Temple came off as a woman who would have a padlock on more than her bedroom door. And his momentary flights of fancy of being locked between those beautiful thighs of hers, and thawing that chilly heart, was a waste of his brain cells. The last thing he was ready for was a tryst with his partner in the middle of a case.

"Plan on wearing your wedding band, Mrs. Morgan?" he asked coming into the living room. "Or are you one of those modern women who doesn't need the shackle of a ring?"

She glanced at him over her shoulder and was two seconds away from rolling her eyes, when she saw what he held in front of his face. His hand was covering those dangerous eyes, palm facing inward. The sparkle of gold from the third finger of his left hand completely caught her off guard. Seeing him with a wedding band on his finger — even if it was fake — unsettled her in a way that she couldn't find the words to explain. She dug in her jacket pocket and pulled out the band that Bernard had given her earlier. For drama's sake she took her time sliding it on her finger. She held up her hand for inspection. "Looks like we're stuck with each other."

There was nothing he loved more than a challenge. A slow grin moved across his mouth. He watched Ashley walk away. Touché, Ms. Temple. Touché. Let's see if you're up for the ride.

CHAPTER 7

Ashley returned to her apartment. She wasn't sure how she felt about the past few hours of her life. The reality that she would be living under the same roof as Elliot Morgan, for an indefinite period of time, was slowly beginning to solidify.

She tossed her purse on the couch, the wedding band that she'd sarcastically flashed at Elliot, picked up the light. She held up her hand. It suddenly felt heavy, as if the enormity of what she was about to embark upon was wrapped round her finger and had real meaning. Don't be silly, she chastised herself. It may be real gold but the union is a sham.

Her cell phone chirped inside her purse. She reached for it, dug around inside and pulled out her phone. "Hello?"

"Hey, it's Elliot."

She took in a sharp breath. "Yes. Is something wrong?"

"Not at all. I know you said back at the apartment that you didn't need any help, but I was planning on renting a small U-Haul to take my stuff and I figured you may as well put your things in there, too. Make the most of the space. Know what I mean? Pretty sure you'll want to take your music. Beats a dozen trips by car."

Why was he being so nice to her? His hot/cold personality was driving her crazy.

"Hello?"

"Oh . . ." she snapped to attention. "Uh, sure . . . I guess. When were you planning on the great escape?"

He chuckled at her quip. "How long will you need to get your things together?"

"I'll need at least a day . . . and I don't mean *to*-day. More like all day tomorrow."

"No problem. I'll get it set up for Saturday. Say around eleven."

Even though he was being the apparent perfect gentleman, his last comment, though couched in a question, was a final statement. Somehow, he'd played the whole scenario out in his head and like a chess master he'd anticipated her response.

Feeling that she'd probably been had, she was of the mind to tell him just what he could do with his U-Haul. But as her grandmother always told her, don't chop off your nose to spite your face.

"How 'bout nine?" she counter-offered, needing some infantile mental leverage.

"Oh, early riser. Nine is fine with me. See you then."

Before she could think of something snarky to say, he'd hung up. Annoyed at herself for being so dim-witted around him she promised herself that she'd be on her game the next time they went head-to-head. She tossed her purse on the couch and stomped off to her bedroom.

Mia, Savannah, Danielle and Ashley sat in their favorite booth at The Shop sipping on mimosas. It was the end of a long day for all of them. Mia had client meetings and site visits all afternoon. Savannah was brain dead from studying for her bar exam, finally taking on the challenge after too much goading from her husband and friends. Danielle had spent the afternoon shooting a bevy of temperamental models for a Victoria's Secret ad. And Ashley had spent her day sorting through her belongings and deciding what to take to her new abode. The girls had agreed to help her pack once they'd had some food and a drink under their belts.

"To a relaxing weekend," Savannah said,

on an exhausted breath, raising her glass in a toast. Her sister friends did likewise.

"Since Ashley is so embroiled in her 'arranged marriage,' " Danielle quipped, winking at Ashley, "I took the liberty of looking up this Elliot Morgan who has our girl's panties all in a knot."

"He does not!" Ashley weakly protested.

"Anyway," Danielle continued drolly, before ceremoniously pulling out her iPhone. She moved her finger around on the touch screen until she found what she was looking for. She turned the phone to face her friends. "Behold, Mr. Elliot Morgan."

A series of wide-eyed oohs and ahhhs, hopped around the table.

"Whoa, now that's what I'm talking about," Mia said squinting at the full-color head-and-shoulder shot.

Savannah nudged her. "Put your glasses on. He'll look even better."

"Very funny," Mia snapped, notorious for refusing to wear her glasses in public, which had become the standing joke between her friends.

"Hey, ladies. I heard the best of the best were going to be here," Traci said in greeting, stealing the line from *Top Gun.*

"Hey, T," they chorused, welcoming the

newest member to the table and their sister-hood. Traci Bennett originally known as Brenda Forde to the girls, had been an agent of Jean's years earlier. She'd managed to leave The Cartel and started a new life, and had Mia not been assigned to uncover an elite escort service run by her former boss and lover Matthew Burke, Traci's identity may have remained secret forever. She'd been Matthew's personal assistant at Avante Management and it was with her help that Mia was able to crack the case.

"What did I miss?" Traci asked as she slid into the booth.

"Mimosas and a picture of Ashley's new man," Danielle teased, which earned her a poke from Ashley.

Danielle giggled and passed the iPhone to Traci.

"Wow. You lucked out, my sister."

"Yes, but as the saying goes, you don't have to live with him."

Savannah leaned forward. "Come on. How bad could it be?"

Ashley sighed. "I don't know," she admitted. "I'm sure my imagination is making it out to be worse than it could ever possibly be. I . . . just . . ." she hesitated, hunting for the right words to describe her confusion. "He's . . . forget it." She looked from one to the other. "Let's eat. *We* have packing to do."

They ordered, talked, caught up with ongoing Cartel cases and one another's lives then headed over to Ashley's apartment.

"The apartment is unbelievable," Ashley was saying as she went through her closet.

"I'll have to start working on your house-warming party," Mia said as she folded and placed clothes in Ashley's suitcase.

Ashley stopped what she was doing and turned to Mia. "This case bothers me," she said, her voice low and intimate.

Mia sat on the edge of the bed. "You want to talk about it?"

"It's . . . I just wonder why Jean picked me. You know she always has a rhyme or a reason for everything she does. Nothing is random or coincidental."

"She assigns people to cases to either force them to prove themselves, test their loyalty or help them to discover their strength," Mia said.

Exactly, she thought. What is it for me? Her honey-brown eyes were almost pleading for an answer that she knew Mia couldn't give. *What is it that Jean knows about me?*

The girls did their inventory of Ashley's

belongings and a thorough inspection of Elliot as he lifted boxes and bags onto the back of the U-Haul rig. They all but fell over each other, helping him and trying to make small talk, which meant uncovering his entire life in twenty minutes or less.

Elliot remained cordial and mildly amused at Ashley's protectors. But he admired their loyalty and concern for their friend, which elevated Ashley in his eyes. She was obviously a woman worth caring about. Even though he didn't have the time nor the inclination to get involved and deeply care about anyone other than himself and whatever he needed to get done.

He shut the door to the truck and turned to face five sets of evaluating eyes. They were all fabulous-looking women — from Traci with her smooth sophistication to Savannah with her petite sexiness. Danielle's avant garde allure to Mia's earthy sensuality. But Ashley was the one who gave him pause. She was wild and tame, spicy and sweet, mysterious and open all rolled into one delicious package.

"That's about it. Thanks for all your help, ladies." He leaned against the van letting his gaze bounce from one to the other.

Ashley stepped away from her crew and walked toward Elliot. "Thanks," she softly.

He looked down into her eyes and he'd swear something jumped in his gut. He ran his tongue across his bottom lip. "Not a problem. I guess you'll drive your car?"

She nodded her head. "I'll follow you."

He lifted his chin in the direction of the quartet. "Will your friends be joining us?"

Ashley glanced over her shoulder and bit back a laugh as she peeked at the expectant faces of her friends. She turned back to Elliot. "Maybe next time."

Their gazes connected, then darted away. Elliot walked to the front of the van then got in his car that was hitched to the front.

"I'll see you all later," Ashley called out, blowing kisses and waving as she opened her car door and got in. "Thanks for all your help." She pulled out behind Elliot. A tingle of anticipation and something akin to fear warmed her insides.

CHAPTER 8

It took them countless "excuse mes," "thanks," "no problems," and several hours to unpack and get relatively settled. They found themselves face-to-face in the center of the living room.

"All done?" Ashley asked on a breath, her hands hugging her hips.

"Yeah, how 'bout you?"

"Almost like home," she said in jest.

Elliot gave a half smile. "I was going to check out the fully stocked fridge. Hungry?"

Her stomach rumbled in response. "Starved."

He led the way to the kitchen and they checked the refrigerator and cabinets.

"I make a mean steak," Elliot said, pulling a package of sirloin from the freezer.

"Sounds like a plan."

They worked together in a comfortable silence, only interrupted by the click of cutlery, running water and Elliot's humming. Every now and again Ashley picked up on a tune he was humming and smiled, humming along with him. The vibe between them and the space they shared seemed as if this was the way it always had been between them.

Unconsciously Ashley squished the tomato that she'd held between her fingers when that singular revelation hit her. This was a job, not some reality TV show, she reminded herself, looking down at the minor mess she'd made on the counter. She stole a glance at Elliot who was putting the steaks in the oven. She drew in a long breath. Get it together, girl. She returned her concentration on finishing the salad that would round out their steak and potato dinner.

"There's wine in that cabinet by the window," Ashley said as they sat down to eat.

"I pass. I'll have a beer. Wine messes with my head."

Ashley grinned. "You're kidding, big strong guy like you."

He shrugged helplessly as he got up. "My Achilles' heel, what can I tell ya." He opened the fridge and held up a Coors, pointing the top in her direction.

"Sure, why not?"

He took out another bottle and returned

to the table.

"The truth is," Ashley admitted, twisting off the top, "wine gives me a headache."

Elliot tapped his bottle to hers in a toast.

"So how long have you been working with Jean?" Elliot asked, cutting into his steak.

Ashley's finely arched brows rose for an instant as she thought about it. "Hmmm. It will be three years next January."

"How were you recruited?"

"I was working for a marketing consortium as a consultant and one of my coworkers, Mae Lin, took me aside one day and told me bits and pieces about the organization and what she did. She told me I'd be great at it because I was always looking for the next challenge." Ashley grinned. "I was intrigued. She said it was like being in a secret sorority with cool gadgets to play with. But that the work was serious and when government agencies didn't have the manpower, the interest or the time, The Cartel steps in. She introduced me to Jean and —" she shrugged her right shoulder "— the rest is history."

Elliot leaned back and took a long swallow of beer. "Where is Mae Lin, now?"

Ashley smiled. "She's a news correspondent on *CBS News*."

Elliot's eyes widened in surprised amusement. "Say what? That Mae Lin?"

Ashley bobbed her head. "Yep. Cartel members are everywhere, doing everyday jobs and no one is the wiser. That's the beauty of the organization. Some of us know each other, but most of us don't, unless we meet during an assignment."

"Jean definitely runs a tight operation. The honchos at The Bureau and CIA headquarters think very highly of her."

"What is your story?" Ashley said.

His expression sobered. "Went to the navy after high school. Figured it was the only way I could afford a college education and get off the streets. I grew up in Baltimore, around where they used to film *The Wire*." He drew in a long breath and gazed off into the distance. "The things I saw in combat couldn't compare to life on the streets of Baltimore, especially back then." His hand tightened around the bottle neck. "I signed up for Special Ops. Stayed there for five years before I signed up with the FBI, which is where I met Bernard."

"I didn't know that the FBI handled cases outside of the U.S."

Elliot's dark eyes flashed at her. His body coiled as if ready to strike, making her heart lurch. In that instant she again witnessed how volatile Elliot could be with just a flip of the switch. "Jean and Bernard told me you were returning from an assignment in Europe . . ." she quickly added, hoping to snuff out whatever fire she'd lit.

By degrees she watched him physically relax, but his eyes remained wary.

"Let's say that I'm freelance and leave it at that. Okay?" He finished off his beer, pushed back from the table and took his dishes to the sink, rinsed, and then put them in the dishwasher. He turned to Ashley. "I'm going out for a while." He left without another word or a backward glance.

"Well, damn," she muttered in concert with the closing front door.

Elliot got in his car with no real destination in mind. All he was sure of was that he needed some space, some air between him and Ashley. He could feel the powder key of his emotions getting ready to explode and Ashley didn't deserve to be on the receiving end of that.

He glanced at the digital clock on the dash. It was still early. He hit speed dial on his cell phone. After three rings, Carmen Santiago's throaty voice filtered through the lines.

"Hello Carmen, it's E. You busy?"

"No. You in the vicinity?"

"I can be in about thirty minutes."

"I'm here."

"See you in a few."

He made a turn onto the West Side Highway and headed to Brooklyn.

After cruising around for about ten minutes, Elliot found a parking space and then walked back the half block. He jogged up the steps to the parlor floor apartment of the three-story brownstone and rang the bell. Moments later the glass and mahogany wood door opened and Carmen stood in the doorway. He felt suddenly lighter.

"Come on in, babe." She welcomed him on tip toe and embraced him in a warm hug.

Elliot kissed her cheek and gave her a squeeze. "Girls asleep?"

"They're at a sleepover down the block. Friends from school."

"Wow. Sorry I missed them."

"Next time. Can I get you anything? I have some Coors in the fridge."

"Perfect."

"Be right back." She sauntered off barefoot to the kitchen in her oversized army T-shirt that hit her at mid-thigh.

Carmen was all of five foot two; compact, gorgeous and dangerous. She could easily take down a man twice her size in hand-to-hand combat. They'd met years earlier while they were stationed in Taiwan on assignment. Against all odds they actually became friends, confidantes. But the stress of her job was putting a strain on her marriage and after six years in Special Ops, she quit to be a full-time wife and mother. It took a while for Phil to accept and believe that there was nothing going on between Elliot and his wife.

There is a bond that forms between people when their lives are in danger and they depend on each other for survival. But the only thing Carmen was more devoted to than her job was her husband and their two daughters. When she lost Phil during 911, Elliot was there for her every step of the way and became a surrogate father to Jasmine and Petra.

"Here ya go," she said bouncing back into the room. She handed him the Coors, then plopped down on the love seat and tucked her legs beneath her. She pushed several curly ringlets of inky black hair behind her ears, revealing tiny gold studs. "So what's going on? How are you?" she quizzed, her dark eyes sparkling and deep dimples flashing. Behind the sexy, pixie image Carmen could run a mile flat out in under five, was as accurate with a long-range rifle as she was with a .45 with a silencer. It was what made her so effective and efficient at her job. She took every enemy by surprise.

Elliot brought the bottle to his lips and drank slowly. "Still trying to get my legs under me from the last assignment. But they have me right back in the saddle."

"Are you okay with it?" she asked softly.

He looked into the gentle sincerity of her eyes. "The assignment, yeah."

"So what's the problem? I know you didn't drive your fine self all the way over her on a big Saturday night to tell me that all is well in Elliot Morgan's world."

He tossed his head back and laughed then leaned forward, resting his arms on his muscled thighs. "I have a partner. A woman. A beautiful, intelligent, funny woman." He took a sip of his beer. "She reminds me of Lynn."

"Oh . . ." Carmen expelled on a soft breath. She hated that witch. Not because she was beautiful and smart and funny and crazy in love with E. No, it was because of what his losing her did to him.

Lynn McKnight was like morning mist, you couldn't really see how it got there but it was all over everything, clinging, and then it was gone. She'd seeped into Elliot's pores, massaged his heart and stole a piece of his soul. He was ready to give everything up for her and live a regular life. Then the most unimaginable tragedy occurred while they were both stationed overseas. Elliot was devastated.

Losing Lynn turned Elliot into a different man; one who lived on the edge, was hard and indifferent, who limited his contact with others and had a woman only to satisfy his physical needs. So if he was in her living room talking about a woman, maybe her prayers were finally answered and he had returned to the land of the living.

"There is only one Lynn McKnight," Carmen said, not falling into the melancholy trap. "So why does she remind you of Lynn?"

Elliot eased back into the couch, contemplating the question, trying to find the words to express his emotions, which was almost foreign to his nature. He looked at Carmen who waited expectantly.

"It's not something that's tangible. It's not physical similarities or even personality," he said, growing frustrated. "It's how . . . she . . ." he ran his hand across his close-cut hair then shook his head slowly. "I don't know what it is," he grumbled.

Carmen smiled softly and threaded her fingers together on her lap. "Could simply be that she makes you feel something, E. Something beyond the next drama of our crazy lives."

Elliot chuckled. "You're probably right. I've been alone inside and out for a long time, Carm. The idea of feeling anything for anybody kinda blind-sided me."

"That's usually the way it happens," she said with a grin. "It may be something and it may turn out to be nothing more than a momentary thrill." She studied his expression for a moment, the hard lines of his face, the taut physique, soulful eyes and that indescribable aura that floated around him. She knew all too well what the job could do to you. It made you cautious, leery of friendships. As operatives you lived with the never-ending suspicion that no one is who they claim to be. So when you do open that door and take a chance on letting someone in and they hurt or betray you, it only reconfirms what you have been trained to believe. "So tell me about the assignment."

Elliot drew in breath that easily helped him slip into his tactician persona, doling out facts, analyzing the information and not missing a beat.

They talked long into the night, bringing each other up to speed on their lives, their concerns about what was happening in the

White House, the kids, mutual acquaintances and everything in between. They ordered pizza from Papa John's and as night drew closer to daybreak, Elliot knew he'd had one beer too many to make the trip safely back to Manhattan and crashed on Carmen's couch, just like in the old days.

He awoke the following morning to the scent of fresh brewed coffee and biscuits, and two pairs of sparkling brown eyes.

"Sssh, see I told you not wake him," Jasmine whispered, nudging her younger sister in the side.

"Ouch! I'm telling. Uncle E, she hit me," Petra whined, pointing an accusing finger at her sister.

Before either of them could react, he leaped from the couch, scooped them up into his arms and spun them around until they were delirious with laughter then unceremoniously dumped them on the couch, much to their delight.

"What is going on in here?" Carmen demanded with a faux frown on her face. She balanced coffee and warm biscuits on a tray. She set it down on the table.

Both girls looked at their mother with wide-eyed innocence.

"Never mind," she conceded. She turned to Elliot. "Sleep okay?"

He stretched. "Nothing that a hot shower won't cure," he joked. "And some hugs and kisses from my favorite girls," he said, diving toward them and tickling their ribs. The room filled with squealing laughter.

Carmen shook her head. "There's everything you need in the bathroom."

"Yes, ma'am." He filled his mug with coffee then tossed a warning look at Jasmine and Petra. "I'm coming back to get both of you," he said, wagging a finger, which only sent them into another fit of girlish giggles. He snatched up a biscuit from the tray and headed to the bathroom.

"Let's go, ladies, breakfast is on the table." She hustled the girls off to the kitchen and for a moment lost herself in the sensation of having a man around again, which gave her all the more incentive to check out this woman who'd gotten Elliot's attention. She still had friends in all the right places that would be willing to do her a favor for old times' sake.

Several hours later, after swearing on the girls' SpongeBob blanket that he would come and see them soon, Elliot said his goodbyes and began the return trip to Brooklyn and his new home. Spending time with Carmen and the girls had done his mind and spirit a world of good, he thought as he cruised through the early Sunday afternoon traffic of churchgoers. He wondered if Ashley went to church, what she believed in, if anything. He pushed those kinds of thoughts out of his consciousness. As Carmen had said while they talked last night, the main thing to remember is that this is about the job. *Sure, get to know her,* she'd advised, *but at the same time you can't let it cloud what you were assigned to do. And if there is any real vibe going on between you two, there's always time afterward to pursue it.*

She was right, of course, as she was about most things that had anything to do with dealing with people on a real level. At least through it all she'd maintained that part of her humanity. She had her children, which compelled her to feel, to care about someone other than herself. He didn't have that. And when his human side dared to make an appearance, he did all he could to stomp it back in place. It was a lonely life, but one that he'd grown accustomed to. It was simply easier that way. It was a lesson he'd learned the hard way. And if there was one thing you could count on when you dealt with Elliot Morgan, you never had to worry about him falling for the same thing twice.

CHAPTER 9

Ashley didn't know whether she should feel pissed off, disinterested or totally dissed by Elliot. They hadn't spent a full day together as "man and wife" and already he was spending the night out. What did that say about her appeal? she wondered morosely. She would laugh at the absurdity of it all, but the truth of the matter was she was actually annoyed. She realized much of it had to do with her lack of sleep. For the better part of the night she kept listening for Elliot's key in the door. That fact added to her annoyance on top of the *other* fact that she was up listening for him in the first place! Even in his absence, he was a thorn in her side. Well, her plan was to pluck the thorn and get on about the business of the case. She didn't care if Elliot Morgan spent every night out. That meant more room for her in the fabulous apartment. *Was he with another woman? Don't even go there,* she warned herself. It didn't matter if he was. *Did it?*

Shaking her head to dispel her roving thoughts, she went into her bedroom, retrieved her laptop and set up in the living room. Hunting through her pared-down collection of CDs, she selected *Blue Magic's Greatest Hits, Marvin Gaye Live,* Jill Scott, Kem and her new favorite, Chrisette Michele's *Epiphany.*

Settling down, she booted up her computer and opened up the information from her flash drive. Within seconds the list of adoption agencies and fertility clinics appeared on the screen. She began sorting them by geographic area and plugging them into her Google map, which she would sync to her PDA later. There were more than seventy locations to check out and no real way to determine which was more important than the other. Just as she opened another file to get the backgrounds on the parents, she heard the lock being jiggled in the front door. Her pulse began to race and her stomach knotted.

The front door opened and she heard heavy footsteps walking down the hallway in her direction. She looked a mess, she realized in alarm. She had on a baggy T-shirt and an old pair of sweat pants. She made a move to dart off to her room, but it was too late.

"Hello," he greeted without enthusiasm. His gaze settled on her for a minute and moved away.

Ashley pretended not to notice him. She studied the files in front of her, but couldn't make out anything that they said.

Elliot moved farther into the room. He stopped in front of her and looked down at the papers spread out across the table. "Are those the case files?"

"Yes, I thought it best that I get started," she said a bit more sharply than she intended.

He came around the table and sat down next to her. The manly scent of him rushed to her senses. She tried to ignore him, but she could feel the heat from his body press against her own. He reached across the table for the file, and his hand brushed against her arm. It was like an electric shock and she jumped as if she'd been struck.

"Something wrong," he asked.

"No I'm fine," she snapped. "Why, is something wrong with you?"

He looked at her from the corner of his eyes. "We're a little testy today, aren't we?"

Ashley jumped up from her seat. She spun toward him, her hands on her hips. "We're supposed to be working on this assignment, and you decide to spend the entire night out!" She knew she sounded like a nagging wife, but she couldn't seem to help herself. She had no right to be upset. He was entitled to live his life anyway that he saw fit. She couldn't seem to control the emotions that tumbled within her.

"Look, I'm sorry about last night. I just needed to get out and clear my head. Went to see a friend."

Her heart pounded in her chest. *A friend?* She wouldn't dare ask him who it was. She didn't need to know. "Fine. You can do whatever you want. But we have a job to do."

"Then let's do it." His gaze held her in place for a moment.

She pushed out a breath of exasperation and slowly returned to her place on the couch. "I've broken down the list according to geographic areas. I thought it would be a good way to get started. That way we can visit specific areas at one time."

Elliot nodded as he looked at her notes. He had to admit, had it been him he would've gone about it the same way. He admired her forward thinking. "That makes plenty of sense to me. What we need to do now is get the names of the heads of all of these organizations. That way we'll know who we're going to be asking for when we show up for our appointment as Mr. and Mrs. Morgan."

Her skin warmed at the mention of "Mr. and Mrs. Morgan." She pretended that she didn't hear him and proceeded to explain that she had the list of names already.

"You have been a busy bee today, haven't you?" A small smile moved around the corners of his mouth.

Ashley dared to look at him and she'd swear she saw admiration in his eyes. "It's what I do," she said, turning back to the task at hand.

"I'm thinking we should start with the fertility clinics," Elliot said.

"I was thinking the same thing," she said.

"So, starting tomorrow morning we'll begin with the fertility clinics until we exhaust the entire list."

"I had no idea there were so many fertility clinics in New York."

"Guess there are a lot of people wanting babies," he said, his voice dropping an octave.

Ashley stared at the screen and thought about her parents and their twenty years of heartache. Yes, she fully understood how desperately parents can want a child, especially a child who had been stolen from them. The desire never leaves. The hole in your heart never gets filled. It's a never-ending ache, and you wake up every day and pray that this will be a better day, a different day, and that all the days before never happened. But then you realize that it has happened. And you are powerless to change anything.

Elliot gently touched her shoulder and felt her stiffen beneath his fingertips. "Are you okay?" he asked softly.

She swallowed over the sudden knot in her throat. She nodded her head. "Yes, I'm fine." Gentleness was the last thing she needed from him, the last thing she wanted. She couldn't handle it, not now. "Let's get back to this list," she said, trying to regain her composure, which was extremely difficult with him being so close, touching her.

Elliot slowly removed his hand from her shoulder. "Yeah, let's. We'll start with the Upper East Side clinics and work our way across town."

For the next hour they worked on developing their list. They knew they'd probably have to make appointments with all of these clinics. But their hope was that they could at least do a walk-in and get some brochures, talk to a couple of the employees and take a look around. One of their goals was to gain access to the clinics' databases. In order to do that, one of them would have to distract the receptionist or whoever was behind the computers. If that failed, they would have to try to plant a micro camera that was focused on the computer screen and on the keyboard. That way the camera could record the keystrokes and possibly access any passwords that were needed to get into the files. Once that was done, they would be able to pass that information along to Jasmine over at Cartel headquarters. She would then be able to download the files they needed. What they were looking for were client lists, the names and addresses of all the couples who had come to the clinics. It would all take luck and timing. And most important, their ability to work together.

Elliot leaned back from his slumped-over position and rotated his stiff neck. "I think that's about all we can do with what we have so far."

"You're right. My eyes are beginning to cross anyway." She saved all of the information they had compiled and closed down the computer.

Elliot stood, and the first thought that

came to her mind was that he was getting ready to leave again. And it annoyed her that she cared one way or the other.

"I think we deserve a treat," he said, "for all the work that we've accomplished."

"A treat?"

"Yeah." He checked his watch. "It's still pretty early. Wanna go explore the neighborhood?"

"You call that a treat?" she asked in a teasing tone.

Elliot chuckled. "What if I bought you some ice cream to go along with the tour? Would that make you feel better?"

She smiled. "Butter pecan can do wonders."

"You're on."

Ashley got up and stretched tight limbs. "Then let me at least change and put on something halfway decent."

"I don't think you need to."

Their gazes connected and that hot sensation exploded in the center of her chest. "Even if you think so, I'm still going to change my clothes."

Elliot shrugged. "Your call. I think you look fine, but I guess it's not for me to say." He turned and walked away.

Ashley stood there for moment vacillating between feeling utterly ridiculous and aggravated once again. It was totally exhausting trying to figure out Elliot Morgan. She headed off toward her room in search of something to put on.

Nearly a half hour later, Ashley emerged in a new outfit. She'd selected a long-sleeved white oxford blouse and a pair of tight-fitting black jeans belted at the waist with a black-and-silver scarf that was knotted and hung down to her knees running along her left side. Since he said they'd be walking she decided to put on her sneakers instead of her boots. She wasn't one to generally use makeup, but she did decide to brighten her eyes with a brush of mascara and bring out her full lips with a touch of gloss. She'd run her fingers through her hair to get the wild and carefree look that she liked. A double-stranded silver chain hung from her slender neck.

"Ready," she announced. Elliot turned from his perusal of the CDs that were stacked up on the entertainment unit. For an instant his eyes widened when he saw her.

She waited for him to comment on her appearance. But he didn't utter a word.

"You need a jacket," he said offhandedly and headed toward the door.

Ashley rolled her eyes, snatched up her

jacket from the hall closet and followed him out.

"If I remember the neighborhood," Elliot said, once they'd stepped outside, "there's a Baskin-Robbins about three blocks away."

"I can wait," she said, falling into step next to him.

"I just don't want you to think I'm not a man of my word."

"You haven't given me a reason to think that — at least not yet."

"And I don't plan to." He took her hand and his large fingers wrapped around hers. Her heart felt as if it had short-circuited in her chest. For an instant her knees wobbled. She tried to pretend that holding Elliot's hand was something that she always did.

"We might as well look like the happy married couple. Shouldn't we?" He stole a look at her.

"Of course," she said, her voice sounding almost unrecognizable to her ears. "We have to keep up appearances."

"Exactly," he said, tightening his grasp around her hand.

As they walked, the tension that had taken hold of Ashley's body slowly began to loosen. She felt herself begin to relax and enjoy the closeness of Elliot next to her.

"This is an amazing city," he said.

"There's always something to do, stores open twenty-four hours a day, night clubs, restaurants, anything that you could possibly want is contained on this tiny little island of Manhattan."

"Yep, the city that never sleeps."

"Do you get to go out much?" he asked.

"Not as much as I would like. What about you?"

"I've been away so long I feel like a tourist." He paused a moment. "About last night . . ."

"Listen, you're a big boy. You don't have to explain anything to me."

"I know I don't, but I want to."

Ashley glanced up at him. He looked straight ahead.

"This is all new to me. This whole thing about working with a partner. Moving in with somebody. It's not something that I'm used to or what I expected — started to rub me the wrong way, and I didn't want to take it out on you. I needed a little space and some breathing room. So I went uptown to see a friend of mine from back in my Special Op days. Maybe you'll get to meet her one day."

So it *was* a woman, she thought. "As long as you're feeling better, that's what's important." She pulled her hand away from his and made busywork of looking in her purse — for what, she didn't know. The only thing she was sure of at the moment was that she didn't want him to touch her. She found a pack of gum at the bottom of her purse and pulled it out. "What one?" she asked, offering him a stick.

"Sure. Thanks."

Ashley put a piece of gum in her mouth to keep her from saying something utterly ridiculous.

"It should be up on this next block," he said, tossing the foil wrapper in the corner trash basket.

They reached Baskin-Robbins and Elliot placed their orders for two butter pecan cones then they continued on their walk.

"If I remember correctly from the notes," Ashley said. "I think one of those adoption agencies is about two blocks away." She took her PDA out of her purse, turned it on and pulled up the data that she'd recently updated. She scrolled down the list of adoption agencies. "Here it is. Happy Homes Adoption Agency. It's two blocks away on 119th Street and Amsterdam Avenue."

"Let's take a look," Elliot said.

"It's probably closed."

"No harm in trying. We might get lucky."

They picked up their pace and quickly covered the distance to the agency. When they arrived they were surprised to see it was open. A young couple was walking out just as they approached.

Ashley and Elliot gave each other a questioning look.

"I'm game, if you are," Ashley said.

Elliot held up his ring finger and the gold band sparkled in the light.

Ashley pinched her lips together and dug in her purse for her wallet. She took her ring out and slipped it on. *Damn, it fit perfectly.* "I was a Girl Scout," she quipped. "Always prepared."

The right corner of his mouth curved upward. "Then you do the talking. I'll follow your lead," he said, surprising himself with his impromptu willingness to give up control.

Ashley gave a short nod of her head, tried to visualize what she would encounter on the other side of the revolving doors. They hadn't had time to run through what their cover story was going to be or practice their conversation strategy. But now she'd see if Elliot was as good as he claimed to be. "Ready?" she asked, looking up at him and not expecting the jolt that danced in her veins.

He took her hand. "Let's pretend we like each other," he said before moving toward the front door.

Ashley started to snap back a tart retort but he was holding the door open and smiling as if he treated her with kid gloves every day.

She crossed the threshold and felt Elliot's heat right behind her.

"Reception, twelve o'clock," he whispered into her hair.

She turned and spoke to him through clenched teeth. "Don't start talking like that. It's ridiculous," she said before she noticed the barely controlled merriment on his face. He was determined to make her crazy. That's all there was to it.

Elliot put his arm possessively around her waist and drew her close so that their hips bumped when they walked.

"It's okay, baby, we're just going to ask some questions," he said, catching her off guard but loud enough to catch the attention of the young woman behind the desk, which was apparently his intention. What happened to her taking the lead?

"Good afternoon. How can I help you?" the young blonde asked from behind the security of the horseshoe-shaped desk.

The front reception area was warm and

inviting. The off-white walls were dotted with framed photographs of loving-looking couples with chubby-cheeked babies. The desk was adorned with small racks of brochures featuring information on adoption, options and referral services.

Elliot tightened his hold around Ashley's waist. "My wife and I —" he gazed lovingly at Ashley "— wanted to get some information," he said, playing the uncertain-but-doting husband to perfection.

"Of course." She stood up and plucked several brochures from the racks on her desk and handed them to Ashley. "I'm sure you would want to speak with one of our counselors who could explain what we do here and everything that's involved."

"Can we do that today, or do we need an appointment?"

"Yes, you would have to make an appointment. I can do that for you now if you want."

Ashley and Elliot looked at each other for marital confirmation.

"Yes," Ashley said, "we'd like to make an appointment."

"Certainly." She settled back in her seat and stroked a few keys on the computer keyboard. She asked them the basic questions: name, address, insurance information and the reason for the visit. She entered the information into the computer, then looked up at them. "We have Tuesday open. There is a morning at ten, and an evening at six-thirty available with our counselor, Ms. Hastings."

"Evening?" Elliot asked, looking at Ashley for confirmation.

"Evening is fine," she agreed.

The receptionist filled out an appointment card and handed it to Ashley.

"You're all set. Tuesday at six-thirty. Oh, the first visit is consultation. We accept all major credit cards and cash of course, but no personal checks. The consultation is a minimum of one hour, sometimes longer. It's two-hundred and fifty dollars. You'll need to pay that before you see the counselor. So I always suggest that first-timers come at least fifteen minutes early to get any paperwork out of the way." She smiled brightly. "Any questions?"

"No. We're good. Thanks," Elliot said.

"Great then we'll see you on Tuesday."

"Would it be okay if we took a look around?" Ashley asked.

"Not much to see. A few offices, the lab, video room, record room." She shrugged. "That's pretty much it. But if you want to look around feel free. Most of the offices are locked. We only have one doctor on call today."

"I just want to feel comfortable," Ashley said, offering an explanation.

"I can't go with you. I need to cover the front. But you can walk around."

"Thanks." They strolled down the hall.

"Good move asking for a tour," Elliot said.

"Thanks. I figured it was a good opportunity for us to get a sense of the place without all of the foot traffic."

"Do you have your kit with you?" he asked.

"I don't leave home without it," she said referring to her jewels of the trade that included a micro listening device, computer disk, a video camera the size of a pot of lip gloss and of course the standard burglary tools.

Elliot took a few quick pictures of the layout with his cell phone and e-mailed them to himself to upload later.

"Pretty simple space," Ashley said as they retraced their steps to the front desk.

"Thanks a lot," Elliot said when they'd returned.

"Sure," the receptionist said. "If you have any questions, we need to reschedule your appointment. Give us a call. My name is Bernice, by the way. I'll probably see you on Tuesday. It's my late night."

"Thanks for everything, Bernice," Ashley said. "See you Tuesday."

Elliot and Ashley walked out.

"One down," Elliot murmured when they stepped outside.

"We've barely scratched the surface," Ashley said, thinking about the long list of possibilities.

"Don't remind me. What's going to help us put a major dent in this is gaining access to the files."

"I know," she agreed. "It'll be tricky."

"You were really good in there," he said, catching her attention.

She glanced at him briefly as they continued down the street and back to the apartment.

"We make a good team."

Elliot hesitated for a moment. "Yeah, we do."

They returned to the apartment, both feeling very proud of themselves.

"At least we have an idea of the setup," Elliot said as he tossed his jacket across the back of the couch.

Ashley unconsciously picked up the jacket and hung it in the hall closet. "It will definitely make things a little easier." She shut the closet door.

Elliot reserved comment but made a mental note to not leave his clothes laying around in plain sight. It was obviously a pet peeve of hers.

"We should talk about this living arrangement before we get too far into it and really get on each other's nerves," Ashley said.

"Now?"

She raised and lowered her shoulder. "Unless you have plans," she said chuckling to keep the sarcasm out of her voice.

"So talk." He dropped down into a side chair and zeroed in on her, giving her his full attention.

"Well . . . I like my privacy," she began, suddenly unsure what she wanted to say, especially with him staring at her like that.

"No problem. So do I."

"I like order." She folded her arms to ward off the shiver of delight that ran along her limbs when she looked at the fullness of his mouth.

"Uh-huh, what else?"

"I like to play my music. It relaxes me."

"Cool. I like music."

She stiffened. He was patronizing her, and she realized the more she spoke, the more ridiculous she sounded. "Forget it." She spun away in the direction of her room. Before she took a step, the strength and seductive touch of his large hand held her shoulder.

"Wait." Her heart thundered in her chest. She dared to glanced at him over her shoulder. For an instant she saw something soft in his eyes, but just as quickly it was gone.

"I don't like this scenario any more than you do," he said. "But for the time being, we're stuck with each other. The quicker we can get this case resolved, the sooner we can go back to our lives. This place is big enough for us to stay out of each other's way."

Ashley swallowed over the sudden knot in her throat. She lifted her chin. "Fine. My sentiments exactly." She pulled away from him and walked into her room. She plopped down across her bed. She was trembling all over. The heat of his touch still burned her shoulder. What was wrong with her? One minute she couldn't stand the thought of him. The next, she wanted him to kiss or touch her in all the places that had gone unexplored in for far too long.

She pulled herself upright. She knew that part of her frustration and trepidation went beyond Elliot. It was the case itself. It brought to bear the pain that she hadn't shared with anyone. Her family didn't talk about it anymore, but the haunted look still remained in their eyes. The same look was reflected in the eyes of the victimized parents the Cartel was now working for. She wanted to tell him that this was no ordinary case — at least not for her. It was personal. Yet she knew that above all, she could not let her own issues overshadow what she was assigned to do.

She got up and went to the dresser, dove beneath her lingerie and pulled out the twenty-three-year-old photograph.

It was one of those hospital photos. The ones they take of the infants. It was only one of two pictures of Layla. Her parents had one and she had the other.

She ran the tip of her finger over the tiny face. Her chest tightened. Where was she? Was she among the stolen children? Was she happy? Was she still alive? Where was her baby sister?

CHAPTER 10

Elliot sat on the couch, his long legs splayed out in front of him. He leaned his head back and closed his eyes. Instantly Ashley's face came to life behind his closed lids. The soft angles of her face, the wild cotton of her hair, her lips, the scent of her. It was all making him crazy, throwing him off his stride. After Lynn, he'd vowed that he would never again allow himself to become emotional about any woman. It had been eight long years. He stuck by his mantra. Then out of the blue, Ashley Temple gets thrown into his life and suddenly all bets are off.

From the moment he met her all the warning bells started to ring. Since they'd first met he hadn't been able to sleep without thoughts and images of Ashley invading his dreams.

They were powerful, potent, waking him from his sleep with an erection hard enough to break wood. It took everything in him to keep from acting upon all the things that ran through his head. Thankfully prudence always won out. It was dangerous to mix business with pleasure. As a result he did everything in his power to turn his feelings off and push her away.

So far it had been working until a few minutes ago when he touched her just as she turned to look at him. The overwhelming desire to take her in his arms was nearly his undoing. Instead, he resorted to what he knew best, cold indifference. But it wasn't working. The throb between his thighs and the unyielding longing were testaments to that.

His jaw clenched. He pushed himself up from the couch with the intention of taking a cold shower, when what he believed sounded like soft sobs caught his attention. He stopped. Listened. It *was* crying.

Slowly, he walked toward Ashley's room. There it was again. Had he been that much of a bastard that he caused her to cry? His stomach tightened. He stood there for a moment, uncertain of what to do.

Gently, he knocked on the partially opened door. He heard some rustling and sniffling. "Ashley . . . is it okay if I come in?"

A moment of silence hung between them. "Come in," she said softly.

Elliot eased open the door. Ashley's back was slightly turned from him as she swiped at her eyes with the back of her hand.

"What is it?"

He took a tentative step farther into the room and it was as if an alarm went off. Her body jerked in his direction.

Tears still hung in her eyes. Her cinnamon skin was flushed. The depths of her pain rose up from her center, crossed the space between them and grabbed at his heart.

Whatever reservations he may have had dissolved, replaced by his innate instinct to protect. He didn't think about it. His feet moved on their own. He was at her side. His arms were around her. Her heart thumped against his chest. Her sobs wracked her body, and he held her tighter. She seemed to mold herself to him, allowing his strength to become hers.

The walls that they'd erected between them began to crumble, brick by brick until they were exposed, breathing the same air, to the same rhythm of their hearts, wanting the same thing, each other.

Tenderly, Elliot stroked her hair, the strength of her slender neck, the gentle curve of her spine. She sighed at his touch.

The trembling slowed and turned into something else. Her fingers pressed into the muscles of his thighs as he held and stroked her.

Neither dared to say a word for fear of breaking whatever magic spell had been cast upon them.

Elliot leaned back, just far enough to look down into her upturned face. Her eyes held hundreds of questions that his lips wanted to answer. By degrees he lowered his head until he could feel the moisture of her parted lips. And then he touched them with his own and an explosion went off deep in his belly and shot through his veins straight to his head.

He groaned as he took her mouth gently at first, still uncertain of her intentions until he felt her return his kiss, melting into his mouth.

The sweet sounds of her sighs echoed in the room. Her arms rose upward, her hands clasped behind his head, pulling him deeper.

His tongue teased her lips then dipped into the honey sweetness of her mouth.

His hands began to roll along her body, familiarizing himself with the gentle curves he'd only imagined.

The thought of having her consumed him,

clouding his good judgment. A battle of right and wrong ensued. Right won.

Against every carnal instinct that beat inside him he broke the kiss, but he still couldn't let her go.

Her wide, luminous eyes opened and settled on his face, questioning, waiting. He stroked her cheek as his gaze danced across her face.

She lifted the hem of her shirt and pulled it over her head. Her steady gaze dared him to look away and he knew he couldn't.

Her breasts rose in perfect crests above the cup of her bra, beckoning him to touch them. And he did.

His thumbs brushed across the soft flesh, and she whimpered, her lids fluttering like butterfly wings. He leaned down and kissed her there. One then the other.

She clasped the back of his head and pressed him deep against her. Her heart raced so rapidly she became lightheaded with desire.

"Ashley," he moaned against the rise and fall of her breasts.

She scooted back on the bed, pulling him with her until they were stretched out together, she pinned firmly beneath him. She felt the heartbeat of his need throbbing between her parted thighs.

He ground his hips against her and she gasped in delight. He flipped onto his side and unfastened her pants. She wiggled them down over her hips and kicked them away. His eyes steaming with longing, raked over her exposed flesh searing her skin like a hot iron. His fingers trailed along the band of her panties. She trembled as his fingers dipped in and touched her there, the center of her, the hard kernel of her desire. And she was sure she would explode.

She was wet, ready for him and that knowledge nearly sent him over the edge. He tried to think of anything that would keep his mind from what he truly wanted, lest he explode.

Ashley didn't give him that option. She unzipped him and, before he could take a breath, her butter-soft fingers enveloped his shaft. She stroked him in bold firm up-and-down motions until he couldn't stand it any longer.

He pulled away from her and stood up. He looked at her one last time before he turned and walked out of the door.

Stunned and shaking all over Ashley curled up into a knot, her humiliation complete.

What was she thinking? What had she done? She'd never be able to face him again.

She buried her face against her knees. *Oh God,* she inwardly moaned.

She felt more than heard his return. She opened her eyes and Elliot was standing above her.

"I never made it past Cub Scout," he said sheepishly, holding up a foil packet in his hand. "Not always prepared."

She tugged on her bottom lip with her teeth to hold back a smile of relief.

Elliot eased down beside her. His eyes slowly moved over her expectant face. "Are you sure?"

She nodded her head.

Elliot leaned toward her and softly kissed her mouth. "So am I," he murmured. He reached behind her and unsnapped her bra. The lush, heaviness of her breasts rose to meet him. He took one taut nipple into his mouth, running his tongue in teasing laps across its surface.

Shivers of delight coursed along her spine. Her neck arched back, thrusting her chest forward.

Elliot pushed her back against the pillows, raised her hips and freed her of her thong. He played with her, taunted her, dipped his fingers in and out of her wet heat until she begged him to stop, to finish, to start. And he obeyed her every command.

He took the condom package, opened it and rolled the thin sheath down along his length. He turned to her. The pulse in her neck throbbed. Her eyes were dark with desire. He moved gently on top of her, her knees raised, bracing his sides. He lifted up on his knees and cupped her behind in his palms.

When the tip of him pressed against her wet opening, she let out a soft cry. He pushed past the tight ring, and slid deep inside of her.

They both moaned in unison at the sublime sensations that defied words.

Jolts of electricity bounced back and forth between them as Elliot moved smoothly in and out of her.

She raised her legs and wrapped them around his waist, and he was certain that he'd been dropped into heaven.

They moved together as if they'd made love hundreds of times before, understanding instinctively the needs and desires of the other. Yet, the familiar was so new and thrilling, taking them on a journey they'd never before traversed. To heights they'd never reached, to a climax that was beyond surreal, rocking them to their souls.

The experience was so potent, so powerful, that once, not even twice was enough.

They loved, and loved until they were weak and satiated.

CHAPTER 11

Ashley rested her head on Elliot's chest. The steady beat of his heart kept time with hers. She drew in a long breath. The past couple of hours were straight out of a romance novel. The crying damsel in distress succumbs to the charms of the tall, dark and handsome hero. If anyone would have told her this scenario, she would have told them how ridiculous and cliché it all was. But it wasn't. It had happened to her.

Elliot caressed her back and drew her closer to him. He stared up at the ceiling. He'd broken all the rules, both personal and professional. The lines that were once clear were blurry. And he didn't care. That probably disturbed him more than anything else. That and the fact that he'd made love to a woman who was vulnerable. She didn't come to him out of any deep feelings or need, but simply because she was hurt, and it was more than likely his fault. He'd taken advantage of the situation. He never really tried to find out what was wrong. Rather, he let his own needs outweigh good judgment over just being a decent human being.

He squeezed his eyes shut. Nothing good could come of this. They both enjoyed a crazy, sexy romp, but that was it. It couldn't go any further. Besides, when this case was over, there was no telling how far they would send him on his next assignment or for how long. He couldn't become entangled with anyone, Ashley Temple in particular. It would be much too easy to fall for her, and falling for anyone was not his M.O.

"What made you come to my room?" Ashley whispered softly into the darkness that covered them.

Her question momentarily caught him off guard. It was as if she was reading his mind. "I thought I heard you crying." When he didn't get a response, he turned slightly toward her. "Were you?" He could feel her nod her head against his chest. "Do you want to talk about it?"

She inhaled deeply and expelled a shaky breath. "It goes back a long time," she finally said.

"What does?"

"The reason why I was crying." She hesitated, uncertain how much she should say. "It's a long story."

"We have all night."

"It's about the case. I've never told anyone, not even the girls. But this is very personal. I think it's the opportunity I've been praying for. And I can't let The Cartel know that I have my own agenda."

He turned fully toward her, gathered her close against him. "Tell me. I'm listening."

"It happened a long time ago, but it still feels like yesterday. I was just a kid, an only child. I thought I would be the only child all my life. My mother and father gave me everything and then my mother got pregnant and everything changed. My parents were ecstatic. They never thought they could have any more children, and suddenly I wasn't at the center of their universe anymore. This new baby was. It was all that they talked about."

She paused as those days and months ran like a bad movie in her head. "I wanted to be happy, too. But I wasn't. There was a part of me that wished the baby away. I just knew that when it arrived my life would never be the same. I didn't want to share my parents' love with anyone."

Her chest heaved. Elliot stroked her hair. "It's normal to feel that way. Sibling rivalry. I hated my younger brother for years until

129

he got old enough to hang out with."

"I wished her away," she said, her voice laced with an anguish that Elliot couldn't understand. But instinct told him that her story was going to take an ugly turn. This was something more than sibling rivalry.

"When she was born, my dad took me to the hospital to see her. My mom was so happy. I'd never seen her so happy. And I wished her away," she said again. "I wished so hard that it ached inside." Her voice cracked. "And my wish came true."

Elliot frowned in confusion. "What do you mean? What happened?"

"The day she was to come home, the nurse went to bring her to my mother and the baby was gone."

"Gone? What happened?"

"She wasn't in the nursery. She wasn't in any of the bassinets. She was nowhere in the hospital. Someone had taken her."

"Oh, Ashley . . ." His voice dropped off into emptiness.

"To this day no one really knows what happened. My mother . . . had a breakdown. My father turned into a ghost. The police looked for her for two years. Nothing. No trace. No clue. Layla was never seen again."

He squeezed her tight. Felt the wetness of her tears against his chest. "You can't possibly blame yourself. You know better than that."

"The rational part of me knows it. But my heart reminds me of how desperately I didn't want her to be a part of the family. And then she wasn't. I've lived with the ugliness of those feelings for years. And then this case comes up, and the memories get dredged up again."

For several moments, Elliot was at a loss for words. The guilt that Ashley carried, whether real or imagined, was an enormous weight that had chained itself to her like an anchor. "Did the police exhaust every avenue?" he finally asked.

"So they said. There was a blip in the media for a couple of weeks and then that disappeared, too, just like Layla."

"What about videotape, sign-in logs?"

"Twenty-two years ago security was almost non-existent in hospital nurseries. Most casualties were baby mix-ups. A lot has changed since then, but not soon enough."

"Did your family try a private investigator?"

"They tried everything. But between my mother's breakdown, paying a detective, attorney fees and trying to live, my dad pretty much exhausted all of his finances. It wasn't until five years after the fact that the hospital accepted responsibility and agreed to a settlement. Believe me. My folks tried everything."

"You didn't have me," he said, surprising himself with his pronouncement.

"What?" She pushed herself into a sitting position.

"I'm saying I'm going to help you. This case, the information, it's everything you didn't have twenty years ago. And you have my help now."

"Why?" she asked, the disbelief rippling through the single word.

"I want to." He drew in a long breath and released it slowly. "Every case that I have been on throughout my career has always been for the 'good of the government.' It was a job that never touched me beyond the surface. I did what was necessary and moved on." He paused for a moment needing to make sure that he said the right words. "When I got this assignment I felt the same way. Just another job. Get in, get out. Everything looks different now."

"Different?"

"Yeah." He kissed her cool forehead. "Let's get some sleep. We'll talk more in the morning. We have a busy day ahead of us tomorrow."

Ashley sighed in contentment and nestled against the warmth of Elliot's body. It had been a long time since she'd been so open and vulnerable with anyone, letting them in on her darkest secret, her hopes and fears. She closed her eyes and tried to sleep, silently praying that she hadn't made the biggest mistake of her personal and professional life.

CHAPTER 12

Everything seemed different in the light of day, Elliot thought, as he stood under the pulse of the hot shower. Last night with the scent and sensations of Ashley deep in his pores he was liable to say anything. And he did. Truth be told, he was no knight in shining armor. He never had been and had no desire to be one now. But if he was nothing else, he was a man of his word. He wouldn't back down from what he promised to do.

He held his face up to the steamy spray. He'd been a fool to get caught up in her tears. Drawn in by her need. Now he was sure she believed that there was something more to what happened last night than what it really was — just two adults satisfying their basic needs.

He turned off the water. That's the way it had to be, he determined. When this case was over, they would go their separate ways and pick up their lives where they'd left off. Simple.

Elliot wrapped the towel around his waist. If it was so simple, why did it feel so complicated?

Ashley poured her second cup of coffee into her mug and sat down at the kitchen table. She heard the water in the shower stop, and instantly a vision of Elliot's naked body emerged in front of her, rippled and dripping wet. She squirmed in her chair.

There was no question that the sex between them was exquisite. As close to perfection as she'd ever experienced, but that didn't excuse the stupidity of it. She knew better. She'd felt raw inside. She'd needed comfort and he'd been there. They'd taken it further than they should have, and it was her fault. She acted like a cat in heat, disrobing for him, almost daring him to make love to her.

She took a sip of her coffee. But he should have seen how vulnerable she was. He should have walked away.

The more she thought about it, the angrier she grew at herself and at him. She regretted telling him anything about her sister. He'd probably try to use that against her as well. Dammit, she could kick herself.

"Morning."

She jumped, sloshing coffee on the table.

"Sorry. Didn't mean to scare you." He snatched a piece of paper towel from the rack above the sink and wiped up the spill. "Any more coffee?"

"Help yourself." She kept her attention riveted on the designs on the mug. Last night they had so much to say to each other. This morning was a series of awkward silences.

"I thought we'd go over the list this morning and start making the rounds," he said with his back to her.

"Fine." She pushed back from the table and padded off barefoot to her room.

Elliot felt the air leave his body. He leaned against the sink. This is going to be bad, he thought.

Ashley returned to her bedroom to retrieve the files and her laptop then went to the living room. She was in the middle of reviewing one of the clinics on the list, when Elliot appeared in the archway. She kept her attention on the computer screen.

"Since we decided on the upper East side as a starting point, I made a list of the three that we could check out today. I uploaded the information to your PDA."

She'd said all of this without casting even

a glance in his direction, which was fine with him, he thought, although he was a bit stunned by her obvious indifference. It was usually the other way around. But as he took a seat on the end chair, he realized that there was nothing usual about Ashley Temple.

Their alibi was to be that they'd been married for six years and had tried unsuccessfully to have a child. They'd recently moved to New York from Columbus, Mississippi, because some of the best doctors and clinics were in New York. They were still torn between in vitro or adoption.

"I figured we can take my Navigator," Elliot said, sliding his arms through his brown leather jacket.

"Sure." She hunted around in her purse to make sure she had everything that she needed. In the event the opportunity presented itself, she would plant some listening and video devices. Satisfied, she zipped her purse, glanced up and was jolted to see Elliot staring intently at her.

"Something wrong?"

"No. Nothing." He gave a short shake of his head. "Ready?"

She nodded. She draped the strap of her oversized burgundy, leather purse over her shoulder. It was a perfect match to her ankle boots.

Elliot couldn't help but notice the perfect picture she made. Her cream-colored cable-knit sweater that topped an open-collared white blouse, paired with fitted black jeans, expertly defined Ashley's attributes. He may very well notice her, he thought as he pulled the door shut behind him, but she didn't seem interested in giving him the time of day.

Ashley made rocket science out of adjusting her seat and fastening her belt, whatever it took to keep her eyes and mind off of Elliot. This was as close as they'd gotten since he'd left her bed before sunrise. She felt empty and stupid and couldn't stop chastising herself for her actions. She never lost control like that before. What was wrong with her? She had acted like a . . .

"You want to talk . . . about anything?" Elliot asked breaking into her dark train of thought.

She stole a quick glance at him. He was staring straight ahead, and the strong line of his jaw was clearly outlined.

"Not really." She pushed her bag down on her lap and folded her arms on top of it. "I think we covered everything," she added.

The layer of sarcasm wasn't lost on Elliot. "Guess we did," he volleyed back with the same level of feigned indifference.

They spent the balance of the drive in silence, with each of them asking themselves "what went wrong?"

It was just after ten when they pulled up in front of the first location, which was discreetly tucked away on the fifteenth floor of an office building. They went through the drill: answering questions, filling out forms and pretending to be the loving but desperate couple who wanted a baby.

"We'd love a newborn," Ashley had repeated at each stop before looking adoringly into Elliot's dark eyes. He'd squeeze her close then kiss the top of her head and look deep into the counselor's eyes. "Whatever my love wants. Money is no object," he'd emphasize.

By the time they'd reached the last stop for the day, no outsider would doubt that they weren't who they claimed to be.

While Elliot had charmed all of the women with his banter, good looks and make-you-wet smile, Ashley had been able to plant listening devices at all the locations: on the desks of the counselors and at the reception desks. She'd only been able to set up one micro camera, and had almost gotten caught when a young, female clerk walked in on her in the record room.

"I totally got turned around," Ashley sputtered, faking embarrassment. "I thought I was heading for the ladies' room." She laughed nervously.

"The restroom is around the next corridor," the clerk said, looking more frightened than Ashley. "You've really got to get out of here," she urged in a harsh whisper. "It's my fault for leaving the door unlocked. If my boss finds out, I'll lose my job."

Ashley lowered her voice and put a comforting hand on the young woman's shoulder. "Listen, I didn't see you. You didn't see me. It's just between us. I would never want to be one that caused someone to lose their job. Let me know when the corridor is clear and I'll slip out."

The girl went to the door and cracked it open. She looked up and down the hallway and frantically waved for Ashley to leave.

"Thanks," Ashley whispered on her way out.

The young woman bobbed her head and quickly shut the door. For an instant Ashley squeezed her eyes closed, inhaling deeply. She certainly couldn't afford any more close calls like that, she thought, as Elliot braked at the red light. She'd decided to keep that little mishap to herself.

"I don't know about you, but I'm starved," Elliot said. "Want to stop and pick up something or do you have other plans?"

"That sounds fine."

"Chinese, Italian, Thai, West Indian?"

"Hmm, some jerk chicken would sure taste good right about now," she said, imagining the hot spices bursting in her mouth.

"I knew I detected an accent," he said, his tone teasing. He snatched a look in her direction.

"Accent? Me no have no accent, mon," she mimicked, reaching way back in her family tree for her Jamaican roots.

Elliot chuckled. "That was really bad, you know."

Ashley pressed her palm to her chest. "I'm wounded."

"I'll try to make it up to you," he said, his tone suddenly soft and intimate.

Her pulse quickened for an instant. She ran her tongue across her lips. She wasn't going to let him get into her head again. "There's a great West Indian restaurant up on Amsterdam and One-nineteen."

"That's a nice little hop. Nothing closer?"

"I've been going there for years. It's worth

the trip. It's really not far from the apartment, just far from here. And I'm pretty sure we won't find an authentic West Indian restaurant in this neck of the woods."

"Yeah, you're right. Guess I can keep my appetite under control for the drive across town."

Ashley lowered her head and grinned.

"We accomplished a lot for our first day out," Elliot said after a few moments of the returned silence.

"Once we activate all of the devices, hopefully, we'll get a hit."

"The real key will be the Trojan that will upload once we connect with them through e-mail. We'll be able to monitor all of their electronic communications."

If they kept the conversation on work, being in the same space would be bearable, Ashley thought as the Navigator picked up speed along the FDR Drive.

"I want to study each of the agencies," Elliot said when they pulled to a stoplight. "I want to go back at least twenty years, if not earlier, on all of them."

Ashley turned questioning eyes on him.

"I have a gut feeling that if an adoption agency was involved in your sister's abduction, it was right here in New York. We already have a buzz on the one on our list from the FBI. They are all highly trafficked. Almost too much. We need to find the source of their babies."

Her heart pounded as she listened to him, amazed and deeply touched. From the moment she'd opened her eyes that morning and throughout the course of the day, she'd convinced herself that all the pillow talk was just that — talk. She'd decided that Elliot wasn't going to ride in on his white horse and save the day. He'd gotten what he wanted, and so had she. This announcement, however, cast Elliot Morgan in an entirely different light. Maybe she was wrong about him.

"You're still willing to help me?" Uncertainty tightened her voice.

He glanced at her for a moment, caught the glint of hope in her eyes. "I may be a lot of lousy things, but I am a man of my word. If I say I'll do something, I do it."

"Thank you," she muttered, clearly chastised. There were few things worse than questioning a man's integrity.

Elliot gripped the wheel with more force than he intended until the pads of his hands began to burn and the crease in his forehead was so tight he was giving himself a headache. Had he totally been that much of an S.O.B. to make her think that he would back out on his word? If a man had nothing else, it had to be his word. It was his bond. Apparently, Ashley didn't think so.

He inhaled a tight, hot breath. Who was he kidding? He *was* an S.O.B. But he wasn't a liar. He switched on the radio to drown out the silence.

Ashley nearly leaped out of the SUV before it came to a complete stop. The tension had been so stifling that it had sucked up all the air. Her lungs burned as if she'd been running a marathon, and she realized that for long stretches of the ride she was holding her breath — waiting — for what she didn't know.

She pushed through the glass-and-chrome doors and was greeted by the mouth-watering aroma of peas and rice, plantains, stewed chicken, curried and jerk chicken, steamed vegetables and plenty of fast-talking island lingo. Feeling embraced by the familiar, she exhaled the breath that she'd been holding and felt her body begin to relax. She stepped up behind a young man with dreadlocks down to his waist and a red, black and green knit skull cap propped on top of his head.

She smiled as images of her summer trips to her grandparents homeland of Kingston, Jamaica invaded her mind. Poverty and

144

crime intermingled with beautiful weather, crystal-blue water and white sandy beaches. The trips stopped when Layla disappeared.

"What do you recommend," came the deep whispered baritone from behind her.

A sprinkle of goose bumps spread across her neck where she could feel the warmth of his breath touch her there. For a hot minute her mind went totally blank.

"Next!" the girl behind the counter called out, snapping Ashley out of her momentary black out.

Ashley stepped up to the counter and Elliot stood by her side. And then he did the damndest thing. He slid his arm possessively around her waist and pulled her securely against his side, looked down into her astonished eyes and said, "What are you having, baby?" in a voice that was so quiet, so personal, so incredibly intimate that the only thing she could envision was her legs wrapped around his back and the length of him deep inside her; and him looking at her like he was right now, as if she was the most important person in his universe.

She lightly ran her tongue along her bottom lip. He smiled as if that was some sort of invitation and she was jolted back to her senses. She turned away from him. "I'll have the jerk chicken with peas and rice."

"Vegetables or salad?"

"Vegetables."

"Make that two," Elliot piped in, full of cheer.

Ashley pressed her lips tightly together to keep from saying something she might regret.

Elliot paid the tab and carried their purchases back out to the Navigator and Ashley was just as hot as the jerk sauce on her chicken.

"What the hell was that back there?" she blasted him the instant the car doors were closed.

"What was *what* back there?" He stuck the key into the ignition and the eight-cylinder engine purred to life.

"You know exactly *what!* All the huggy, kissy, what are you having, baby. That's what."

She could hear how she sounded — like a nagging wife, the girlfriend that's called a "B" to her face and doesn't care — but she couldn't help herself. Elliot brought out the worst in her.

Elliot eased the SUV into traffic. His jaw tightened. This whole operation was wearing thin, really quick and they'd just gotten started. They'd been at odds since day one and now that they'd slept together it only made a bad situation horrific. "I guess I was still caught up in the charade." He cut a look in her direction. "Show's over. Happy?"

Ashley could almost see the steam rising off the top of Elliot's head. He had every right to be angry. What had he done that was so awful? Touch her? Call her baby? The fault wasn't with him, but how his kindness made her feel when she knew it wasn't and could never be real.

The walls went back up.

When they returned to the apartment Elliot tossed his jacket on the couch, no longer giving a damn whether it pissed her off or not. He took the bag of food and brought it to the kitchen. Setting it on the counter he removed one of the foam containers then grabbed a beer from the fridge. He took everything into the living room and set up camp on the couch. He pointed the remote at the forty-two-inch screen and surfed for something to drown out the past half hour. He settled on an ESPN special "The Championship Knicks."

Ashley didn't say a word. Quietly she retrieved her meal from the bag on the counter and took it to her room. The more distance they put between them at the moment the better, she thought as she closed her room door.

She stared at the food that she'd been salivating over and couldn't take one bite. Instead she sprawled out on her bed and stared up at the ceiling.

When she emerged more than an hour later with the intention of putting away the uneaten food, she realized that the apartment was totally quiet. The living room was empty. She listened for any sounds. Silence. She eased down the hallway toward Elliot's bedroom. His door was open. That room was empty, too.

She dared to step inside. The room was surprisingly neat. The bed was made. All of his clothes were put away. A robe dressed the bottom of the bed and his laptop sat opened on the desk by the window. She walked to his closet and opened the door, ran her hands along his shirts and sweaters. The air held the intoxicating scent of him and for a moment she closed her eyes and inhaled deeply. Wrapping her arms around her waist, she slowly opened her eyes, closed the closet before taking a final look around and walked out.

Elliot contemplated what he was about to do during the entire drive. He didn't see any alternative. He parked the SUV and cut the engine. Before he could convince himself to change his mind, he got out of the vehicle and walked down the quiet tree-lined street. He stood in front of the house for a moment then walked to the door and rang the bell.

Moments later, a surprised Claudia answered the door.

"Elliot!" She pulled the door open. "Is everything all right?"

As always Claudia was impeccably dressed. Her oyster-colored long-sleeved silk sweater over tan slacks, with a thin gold chain at her unlined neck could easily take her from morning to night without missing a beat. Recently wed to Bernard Hassell, Claudia still had the glow of a happy bride.

He leaned down and kissed her cheek. "Everything's fine. I'm sorry. I should have called."

She waved off his apology. "Come in. Come in. I was just surprised to see you. I assume you came to see Bernard?"

"Is he here?"

"Yes, banished to the yard where he's smoking those awful cigars." She wrinkled her nose. "Go on out back."

Elliot grinned. "Thanks." He walked through the sprawling ground floor of the three-story brownstone. The gleaming wood floors reflected the perfectly placed antique furniture and the off-white walls showcased the expensive art that went from Basquiat to Synthia Saint James. He passed through the dining room to the kitchen and walked out the back door.

Bernard was reclining on a blue-and-white-striped lounge chair, sipping on what looked like brandy and puffing happily on his cigar. He looked up when he heard the door squeak and his eyes widened for a moment before a slow smile moved across his mouth.

"Well, well. What brings you to the mountain," he joked, emitting a soft chuckle.

"I need to talk."

Bernard's smile slowly faded. His brows drew close. The sober expression on Elliot's face was a clear signal that this was no ordinary social call. "Sure. Have a seat." He extended his hand in the direction of the second lounger.

Elliot sat on its edge. He folded his hands on his thighs and leaned forward. "I need you to get me off of this assignment."

"I see." He adjusted the collar of his thick zip up sweater to ward off a sudden gust of chilly wind that had started to pick up as the sun began its descent. "You want to tell me why?"

Elliot lowered his head and blew out a

150

breath through puffed cheeks. He looked across at Bernard who regarded him with the patience born of a man who'd grown accustomed to long stories.

"I'm not the one for this job."

Bernard made a noise in his throat. "Of course you are or you wouldn't have been selected. You'll have to do a much better job of convincing me."

Elliot stood, jammed his hands into his jeans pockets and began to pace in front of the George Foreman grill. "You know I don't work well with a partner. Haven't for years."

Bernard didn't respond.

Elliot tried again. "We don't get along. It's a bad mix."

"It's getting a little chilly. Let's go inside." Bernard slowly pulled himself up, his marquee — good looks defying his nearly sixty-years of age. He stamped out his cigar in the ashtray, took what was left of his drink, pushed open the door and led Elliot to his study. Bernard walked toward the window that looked out onto the dimming street. The lights had come on, giving the historic Sugar Hill neighborhood an old-world charm.

Bernard turned and leaned against the sill. He crossed his long legs at the ankles. "I'm still waiting to hear what you could possibly tell me to make me pull you from this case." He folded his arms across his chest. "This isn't high school where you get to pick and choose who you sit next to in class." His voice grew harsh. "Kids are disappearing. Families are being torn apart and you're talking to me about not getting along? You wanna tell me what the hell is really going on? 'Cause what you're telling me ain't cutting it."

"I slept with her," he shouted. "I crossed the damned line." He walked back and forth, ran his hand across his face. His jaw clenched.

"Have a seat," Bernard ordered after watching Elliot weave a trail across the imported Aztec area rug.

Elliot's tortured dark gaze snapped in Bernard's direction. Reluctantly he dropped down into a side chair, leaned on his elbows and pressed his forehead into his palms.

"If you're intention is to shock me, you haven't. Although I must admit I'm a little disappointed that you would be so reckless." He moved away from the window and sat down opposite Elliot. "You want to tell me what happened?"

"Not really. Just that it happened. Compromises everything."

"What does Ashley have to say?"

"We haven't spoken . . . not about that."

"Well, you're going to speak to me. Starting now."

"I know it was a mistake. All right. Maybe it was to keep us from killing each other." A flash of Ashley moaning beneath him filled his head and clouded his vision. The way she whispered his name, filled his ears. The way she felt, made him numb to everything else. The way she made him feel, had brought him to Bernard's door.

"Jean doesn't make mistakes," Bernard stated matter-of-factly.

Elliot's head jerked up. "What?"

"She doesn't make mistakes."

"I heard you the first time. I wanna know what you're talking about."

"Simple. When Jean sets up an operation she examines every eventuality. She's like a master chess player, always three steps ahead, anticipating the next move."

"So I'm being played like some kind of puppet?" he said, his voice rising in disbelief and outrage.

"I wouldn't go that far. You and Ashley were selected specifically for this job, because of your skills and because of who you both are." He gave Elliot a long, hard look, hoping to convey his message. "She's never been wrong. That's why she's so good at what she does. Just do your job, E." He paused. "Look, I know losing Lynn the way you did . . . I know it was hard. She was more than just your partner. But it wasn't your fault. No one could have known about the bomb. Not even you."

The horror of that day would live with him forever. They'd been stationed in Iraq, on a mission to uncover subversives. This was to be their last job. They'd decided to live a "regular" life. They were happy and eager to get the job done so they could return to the States. They'd gone into town the next morning, to the market. The streets were teeming with people, eager for fresh fruits and vegetables. Lynn had left his side to negotiate with the fish monger and then the explosion. The screams. The smoke. The flames. The sirens.

His throat tightened. He'd vowed never again to allow himself to become that attached to anyone, to feel like that about anyone. Since that day, years earlier, he'd worked totally alone. Until now.

Elliot jerked out of his seat. He stared hard at Bernard. "I don't like being manipulated. You can tell Jean I said so. When this thing is over . . . lose my number." He turned and stormed out, barely saying

154

goodbye to Claudia.

Through the window Bernard watched Elliot drive off and wondered if this would be
the first time that Jean was wrong.

CHAPTER 13

When Elliot returned to the apartment, the
achingly soulful sound of Billie Holiday's
"God Bless the Child," greeted him. The
tightness in his chest began to loosen as the
music glided through his veins. He went
through the foyer. The lights in the living
room were muted, but he could make out
Ashley curled up on the couch, a glass of
wine at her feet.

He walked all the way in. She didn't move
and when he looked closer he realized that
she was asleep. He slowly sat down on the
footstool and watched the even rise and fall
of her chest, the way her long lashes fluttered ever so slightly when she breathed.
She looked perfectly angelic, a halo of wild,
cottony hair framing her heart-shaped face.
As if drawn by some unseen force, he
reached out and gently pushed aside a curl
that hung by her eye.

She stirred. Her eyes flickered then

opened fully. When they focused on him, she scrambled to sit up.

"Sorry." He held up his hands. "I didn't mean to wake you."

Ashley ran her hand across her face. "I need to get up anyway." She made a move to stand.

"No." He pressed her thigh with his hand, holding her momentarily in place. "Don't leave."

Her heart banged in her chest. The thigh he just touched felt hot.

"I'm . . . look, I'm sorry for earlier. I was trying to piss you off."

"Oh really. I hadn't noticed."

Elliot gave a short laugh.

They looked at each other and their tense expressions slowly began to soften.

"I have my ways," Elliot began. "It's not personal."

The comment, though made as an appeasement, stung Ashley. She'd been holding on to the false hope that maybe, buried beneath the thick skin, that Elliot had felt something when they'd made love. But they hadn't made love, she corrected herself. They'd had sex. Plain and simple. And she needed to stop being such a "girl" about it and move on.

Ashley straightened up and forced a smile.

"No worries. I finally realized that you were simply being your obnoxious self," she said, nonchalant.

The corner of his mouth lifted. "Touché." He got up, stood over her. "Think I'll take a shower. Long day. Then I'm going to go check the surveillance, see if we picked up anything." He walked out.

Ashley remained where she sat, fighting the urge to throw something. This man had her totally off her game. She needed to get on track and focus. She got up, took her glass from the floor and walked off to the kitchen.

She stood over the sink and washed out her glass. If she was going to focus on the case and possibly uncover information about her sister's abduction, there was no better time than the present. She put the glass in the drain, flipped off the light and began to retrace her steps.

Elliot was coming from his room. The scent of his freshly scrubbed body preceded him.

They met in the center of the apartment, the couch and tables separating them. The hallway light cast them both in shadow.

"Still up?" He tightened the towel around his waist, crossed the open space and walked toward the kitchen. "I have a taste for something," he said opening the fridge and looking deep inside, "just can't figure out what it is." He stood, turned his head and looked at her from above the open door.

Ashley's heart was inexplicably pounding in her chest. He closed the door and she would've sworn that his towel was missing, even though she knew it was just her imagination working overtime.

He stared at her for a long minute. His stomach tightened. *God, you're beautiful.*

"Thank you," she whispered into the security of the semi-darkened room.

Damn! Had he actually spoken his thoughts out loud? Yeah, he was losing it, and quick. He rocked is jaw back and forth trying to think of a wisecrack comeback. He couldn't. He ran his hand across the top of his close-cropped head. Now what?

"Do you mean that?"

Elliot focused on her, thought about his conversation with Carmen and earlier with Bernard. There must be something incredibly special about Ashley Temple that had dragged him out of his self-imposed prison and stripped him of the prickly armor he'd worn for the past six years to keep any and everyone at bay.

"Like I told you earlier, I'm a man of my word."

Ashley's gaze faltered for a moment. "I believe that," she admitted. "And I swear I'm really not the wicked, short-tempered bitch that has taken over my mind. Ask my friends, I'm really likeable," she cried, playfully.

Elliot chuckled. "You definitely need to carry around your references." He waited a beat, enjoying the look of happiness in her eyes. "My friends call me E."

A soft smile lifted her full lips. "Hello, E. My friends call me Ms. Temple," she said with a mischievous light in her eyes.

"Oooh, do they?" he chuckled. He stretched out his hand.

Tentatively, Ashley moved toward him, walking around the table, past the chairs until she stood right in front of him. She looked into his eyes, then down at his hand. She placed her hand in his and his warm fingers closed securely around hers.

"Pleasure to meet you, Ms. Temple."

"Nice to meet you, E."

The thermometer rose from room temperature to sizzle in zero point ten seconds.

Inadvertently her lips parted ever so slightly as she stared into his eyes, seeing the same longing, the same desire that she knew he saw in hers.

Elliot stepped closer, still holding her

hand. "This is crazy." Uncertainty mixed with possibility in his voice.

"I know," she whispered, captured by the caress of his smile. "We're supposed to hate each other."

He stroked her cheek with his fingertip, setting off ripples of delight that shimmied through her body. Her eyes fluttered as she let the sensation have its way with her.

"Hating people doesn't ever feel this good, I can assure you," he uttered, a moment before his warm lips brushed hers.

Her soft moan of pleasure was like finding the key to eternal happiness. Elliot's soul opened to welcome that little piece of joy. This was what he'd been afraid of — this feeling — and then have it taken away. That he knew he couldn't do ever again, but maybe for the moment he could pretend that this feeling was for always.

Elliot pulled her flush against him, his need for her pulsing against the towel that separated them. Her mouth was just as sweet and welcoming, taking him in like one who'd lost their way and had finally found the road home.

Ashley wrapped her arms around his neck, her mouth, her tongue eager to meld and dance with his. For now, nothing else mattered except the inexplicable need that she

161

had for this man that drove her crazy. She didn't understand it, and probably never would. All she knew was what she felt: desire. She knew what she wanted, Elliot.

She gasped in surprise when Elliot suddenly scooped her up into his arms.

"Your room or mine?" he asked, his voice thick and heavy.

"Let's try your bed this time," she answered him in a sultry whisper.

"Say no more." He kissed the tip of her nose, her cheeks, her eyelids as he carried her down the hallway with ease. He pushed open his bedroom door with his foot and crossed the room to his bed in long-legged strides and eased them both down on his king-size bed.

"We'll hate each other in the morning," she said softly, her eyes wide and playful.

"You're probably right," he answered. "But let's not talk about it," he said before taking her lips to his own in a long, deep kiss. Finally he eased back. "Why worry about tomorrow when we have this whole night to concentrate on?" He kissed her again, softly, almost tentative this time as if it was the first.

The gentle exploration was more arousing than when their eager tongues were entwined. Ashley felt herself bloom like a

162

flower awakened by the warmth of the morning sun. Her body grew full as her veins filled with desire and it flowed through her with growing urgency. Every tight muscle loosened. Her thighs eased apart as Elliot's strong and sure hands roamed her lines and curves.

He lifted up and pulled the towel away from his waist. Staring into Ashley's eyes he took her hand and placed it on his hardened shaft. They both moaned at the contact.

"That's how much I want you," he groaned, squeezed his eyes shut when she tightened her hand around him.

The feel of him in her hand was an erotic rush that defied explanation. It gave her a sense of power to know that she could make him feel this way — about her. Slowly she stroked him, feeling the veins and muscles tense and ripple beneath her fingertips.

Elliot groaned deep in his throat, grabbed her hand, squeezed it once, then pulled her hand away from its hold. He eased her back onto the bed, unfastened her pants and pulled them off her, tossing them to the floor. He took off her sweater and it joined her jeans.

He moved up on the bed and turned on the night light. "I want to see you," he said, his gaze searing a trail along her exposed flesh. He removed her panties, inching them down her thighs and across her legs like some sexy cabaret routine. He let his fingers caress her, moving across her stomach until it quivered, her inner thighs until they trembled, and ever so lightly across the perfectly tapered curly triangle that shielded the epicenter of her need.

Ashley moaned and gripped the sheet into her clenched hands when Elliot's thumb pressed her swollen clit. He massaged it until it was rock hard and fully exposed from its protective sheath. She writhed against his ministrations, her hips rising and falling to capture the pleasure that he was putting on her.

And then she was hot, wet, suckled and she cried out in blinding delight as his mouth and tongue intensified what his fingers had done. Her head spun and white light flashed behind her closed lids. Wave after shock wave of pleasure jettisoned through her. She tried to scoot away when the pleasure became so intense that it was almost unbearable. But Elliot had no intention of letting her get away. He gripped her hips, raising them higher, leaving her completely open to him and his hunger, to quench his thirst for her.

Her head thrashed back and forth as his

tongue flicked, laved and teased. Reason left her and all that remained was the driving need for release, which Elliot seemed intent on giving her.

Elliot inserted one finger then another. Ashley groaned but he didn't stop. He spread his fingers inside of her and gently slid them in and out, bringing tears of pleasure to her eyes. Her strangled moans spurred him on, and when her body began to tense, her thighs spread wider and her body open fully to him, he knew that she was on the brink of coming and he wanted to experience it with her.

"Ohhhh," she cried. "Ahhhh . . . E . . . yesss."

"In the drawer," he urged in a voice that was raw and gravelly. "Open it," he ordered as he continued to finger her toward ecstasy.

Barely able to focus, Ashley reached out to the drawer of the nightstand and pulled it open. She felt around inside and found a condom package.

"Put it on me." He pressed his thumb against her clit and her hips rose and bucked against his hand. "Do it." He could already feel the moisture forming on the tip of his penis and he knew it was only sheer will that kept him from climaxing.

Ashley fumbled with the condom pack

and finally got it open. Another wave of electricity shot through her. Her eyes rolled.

Elliot came up on his knees and moved between her parted thighs, keeping his fingers in place. He was rock hard and at full attention.

Ashley rolled the condom over the head and down as far as it would go, which was only halfway.

With his free hand, Elliot pulled her bra down beneath her breasts forcing them higher. Her nipples were hard and full, calling for his attention. He lowered his head and drew the dark grape into his eager mouth and he pushed deep and hard inside her in one swift move.

A whoosh of air expelled from her lungs as her insides instinctively gripped him, the muscles opening and closing around him.

"Ahhhh," he groaned, moving in long, slow strokes willing himself to extend the incredible feeling that rocked them both. He draped her legs over his arms and pushed them back and as far as her body would allow and sunk into the depths of her essence, tapped the spot, once, twice, three times and then heaven and earth collided.

Ashley's entire body undulated in wave after wave of unspeakable explosions, as Elliot rode out his own fantasy, his longings, his wants and needs and finally they merged into one long jet stream of release that erupted within her.

For several joyous moments they bathed in the afterglow, entwined, joined. The rush of their breathing, the pounding of their hearts were the only sounds in the room. By degrees their breathing and racing hearts slowed to normal.

Elliot kissed her along the ridge of her collarbone, making her squirm. "Hate me yet?" he asked, thrusting gently into her as he felt himself growing hard again.

"Not quite," she said, feeling his swelling begin to fill her. She rolled her hips. "Maybe we . . . need to . . . finish working out . . . our aggressions," she said, halting between her words with each of his thrusts.

Elliot suddenly turned onto his back and took her with him, his thoroughly engorged penis binding them together. "Why don't you show me how aggressive you can be," he challenged. He reached up and cupped her breasts in his hands and gently massaged them, teasing the sensitized nipples between the tips of his fingers.

Ashley arched her back and braced her hands behind her on his muscled thighs. She milked him in a mind-blowing climax with quick up and down thrusts of her hips and the deep squeeze of her inner muscles that had them both seeing stars.

Later they lay side by side, the cool sheet covering their damp bodies to the waist. Ashley's insides still quivered and periodically Elliot's shaft jumped. But they both knew that enough was enough for one night.

"Since this is your room, I don't expect that you'll be getting up and leaving in the middle of the night," Ashley said, half in jest.

"I don't plan to." He paused a moment. "And I'm asking you to stay. If you want to."

She turned halfway toward him. "You mean that."

"Yeah," he said after several beats. "I mean it."

"I want to," she whispered.

They were quiet for a while, absorbing the reality behind what had just been said between them.

Ashley tilted her head to press against Elliot's shoulder. Elliot slid his arm beneath her and drew her close to him and he felt warm inside, something he hadn't felt in longer than he cared to remember. It was a comforting sensation, like everything was going to be okay.

"This isn't going to be easy," she said

softly, thinking about the enormity of stepping out in the ocean of a relationship with Elliot Morgan.

Elliot exhaled slowly. "It never is."

She angled her head toward him. "You sound like you have experience," she said, trying to sound light against his suddenly somber tone.

Several moments passed and with each ticking second, Ashley felt the panic rise as if waiting for an impending explosion any minute. And it did.

"Her name was Lynn," he said quietly.

Ashley's heart thumped. She didn't move.

"We met about eight years ago during training." Slowly he told her bits and pieces about his and Lynn's relationship, how they'd gotten together and how he'd lost her.

Listening to him tell her about another woman was difficult to hear, but it explained so much about who Elliot Morgan was and why he lived his life the way he did. This compounded with Bernard's revelations told Elliot's painful story. She understood all too well about loss and the devastating aftereffects it could have. She snuggled closer to him, listened to his heart. Maybe they weren't so completely different after all.

CHAPTER 14

The following morning they sat down at the kitchen table together after having prepared a breakfast fit for a crew of construction workers.

They'd awakened in a tangle of limbs and twisted sheets. Ashley's leg was draped across Elliot's hip, his large hand was clamped securely around her plump bottom. They made slow and easy love, taking their time as if waking in each other's arms was an everyday occurrence. The comfort and familiarity made the experience that much more enjoyable.

After a long, hot, sudsy shower, they both agreed that they were starving and pretty much fixed everything available from omelets to pancakes, turkey sausage, grits with cheese, wheat toast and fruit.

Elliot finished off his second plate and pushed it to the side. "Can't take another bite." He rubbed his stomach.

Ashley grinned. "I was beginning to think you had a bottomless pit down there instead of a stomach."

"Trust me, that's what it felt like." He looked across the table at her and his eyes darkened. "You drained me of all my essence, woman. I had to replenish, build my stamina back up."

"Oh, sure, blame it on the new girl," she joked while she collected the dishes, scraped them and loaded them into the dishwasher.

"I never did get around to checking the surveillance. Seems like the new girl got all of my attention."

"If you ask me, you get distracted much too easy," she said, sashaying past him.

He reached out, grabbed her around her waist and deposited her on his lap amidst a fit of giggles.

"A man is entitled to his distractions," he said cupping her chin and stealing a kiss. "As a matter of fact I feel a distraction coming on now."

Ashley pressed her palms against his chest. "We have a busy day. You have surveillance to check and I have to go to work. I do have a job you know," she added, teasing his lips with flirty kisses.

"It won't take long," he said into the soft hollow of her neck.

Ashley arched her head back to look at him. Her skin began to tingle.

Elliot tugged on his bottom lip with his teeth as he watched indecision transform into action. Ashley reached between them and tugged on the loose knot of the belt on her robe. The soft sea-foam-colored terry robe fell open allowing him to feast on her beauty.

He groaned softly and pressed his face between the swell of her breasts, inhaled the sweet fragrance of her skin until he was dizzy with needing her again.

She stood and the robe dropped from her shoulders. She reached down and freed him from his boxers before slowly lowering herself onto him.

"From now on we have to be fully dressed at the kitchen table," Ashley shouted as she hurried down the hallway to the front door. She snatched her coat from the closet and when she turned, Elliot was right in front of her.

He threaded his fingers through the back of her thick hair and pulled her close up against him. He kissed her until her knees wobbled.

"It never stopped us before," he said against her mouth, while his free hand snaked beneath her blouse to caress her breasts.

She whimpered a weak protest, feeling herself dampening with desire. She grabbed his hand. "E, I have to go."

He ran his tongue along her neck. "I know."

"Then stop," she said, her voice hitching when he tweaked her nipple.

"I can't . . ." He turned her back to the wall and pulled her skirt up around her waist.

"E . . ." she moaned, knowing that her body was betraying her best intentions.

"Ssssh, baby," he hummed in her ear as his hand slid down around the band of her thong and stockings, to find her wet and wanting. "Just what I was looking for," he said, staring deep into her eyes as his fingers dipped in and out of the honey that was her essence.

Ashley stepped out of her heels and it was the last signal that Elliot needed. He took a handful of her stocking and ripped them open from the crotch. Her red thong was about as much of a roadblock as dental floss. He grabbed her and lifted her up, pressed her securely against the wall as she wrapped her legs around him.

■ ■ ■ ■

On still-shaky legs, Ashley finally arrived at MT Management. She'd called Mia from the car to let her know that she'd be late after taking yet another shower — alone — and changing her clothes. They had a meeting with a potential client at eleven and she walked in the door with barely fifteen minutes to spare. She put her purse in her desk, greeting Melody, the new intern, then walked to Mia's office in the back of the ground-floor space. She knocked on the door.

"Come in," Mia called out.

Ashley opened the door and stuck her head in. When Mia looked up and saw her, Ashley would have sworn that there was a big old scarlet letter posted on her forehead for all the world to see. But of course that was ridiculous.

"Hey. 'Morning. Everything, okay? You're never late." She went back to reviewing her file.

Ashley swallowed. "Yeah, I'm fine. Just some things came . . . up this morning."

"Not a problem, the client called just before you got here and needs to push the meeting back until later this afternoon."

"Oh, great," she said, breathing a sigh of relief. "It will give us some time to go over our notes."

MT Management was Mia's dream come true. It was the perfect complement to her personality. She was an obsessive organizer and her attention to detail and planning the perfect event from your basic baby shower to mega corporate getaways was legendary. She knew everyone who was anyone worth knowing to get a job done. Mia Turner's contact list could go on the market for millions, which was why MT Management was the most highly paid, sought after event planning business in New York.

Mia swept her glasses off the bridge of her pert nose and closed the folder in front of her. She waved off Ashley's comment. "We have time to discuss business. You've been off the radar the past couple of days. What's happening with the case and the man you love to hate?"

Ashley tugged at the collar of her blouse.

Mia squinted. "Is something wrong?"

Ashley flashed an awkward smile. "I wouldn't say wrong exactly."

Mia's brows rose. She got up from her desk and went to close the door. She sat back down and buzzed Melody on the intercom. "Mel, hold all my calls for a few minutes, okay."

"Sure thing, Ms. Turner."

Mia turned her attention fully on Ashley. "If you want to talk I'm all ears and I have all day." She waited a beat. "You were there for me through the whole Michael debacle." Her voice softened. "You were the only one I trusted to listen without question or judgment. Not even Savannah or Danielle. I'm willing to do the same, whatever it is."

Ashley drew in a long breath and let it out slowly. "How 'bout if I tell this tale just once?"

Mia's somber expression brightened. "Then, girl, it must be juicy!" She pressed the intercom again. "Mel, do me a favor and call Mr. Archer. Tell him I deeply apologize but we'll have to reschedule at his convenience." She hung up and before Ashley could say a word, Mia had contacted Savannah, Danielle and Traci who all agreed to drop everything and meet her and Ashley at The Shop in an hour.

Ashley simply shook her head and went along for the ride. Once Mia was revved up and had an agenda there was no stopping her. Besides, who better to air her dirty laundry than with her girls.

Danielle and Traci were already at their

booth when Ashley and Mia walked in.

"Hello ladies," they all greeted in unison, buzzing one anothers' cheeks.

"Where's Savannah?" Mia asked, sliding in next to Traci.

"She texted me a few minutes ago, said she was stuck in traffic, but was on her way."

"Guess we can order in the meantime," Mia said.

They flipped open their menus and gave their orders to the waitress, just as Savannah breezed in.

"Sorry I'm late," Savannah said, a bit breathless. She squeezed in next to Mia and blew kisses to everyone. "So what's so pressing to get us all up in The Shop on a Tuesday?" she asked, with a big grin.

"I think sista girl here has some things she needs to get off her chest," Danielle quipped, looking at Ashley.

All eyes turned to Ashley.

She looked from one expectant face to the next. "All right, all right, you beat it out of me. I slept with him."

Four mouths dropped open at the same time but nothing came out.

Traci was the first to recover. "Are we talking about the same man that less than a week ago, you couldn't stand the sight of?"

"You don't have to put it quite like that,"

Ashley said meekly.

"Okay, so how would you put it?" Dani asked.

Ashley swallowed. "It's not that simple."

"It never is, sweetie," Savannah said. She reached out and covered Ashley's hand. "Tell us what you want to, and keep what you don't to yourself," she said gently, always the diplomat.

Ashley pressed her lips together. Slowly she shook her head. "I don't know . . . one minute we at each other's throats and the next we were rolling around in bed . . . in the shower . . . in the chair . . . in the hall . . ." Her voice drifted off as the images of the two of them played in full color in her head making her toes curl right inside her Jimmy Choos.

The quartet's brows were raised so high they all but disappeared into their hairlines.

"Forget about keeping anything to yourself," Danielle finally said. "I want details." Her voice rose two octaves. "In the hall?"

Mia threw Danielle a look.

"What, what did I say?" Danielle asked, looking innocent.

Mia just shook her head.

The waitress arrived with their food.

"You can share my plate," Traci said to Savannah who'd never gotten around to ordering. She pushed the plate between them.

"Can we have a round of mimosas?" Mia asked the waitress before she left the table.

"Make mine a double," Ashley muttered.

Over drinks, good food and friendship, Ashley tried to unravel the story that had suddenly become her life. She told them of the tension that simmered between her and Elliot like a pot of stew ready to boil over. How they'd finally talked, about themselves, life, the world. She told them about Lynn and how it had devastated him, leaving him unwilling and pretty much unable to care about anyone, especially someone that he worked with. And then she told them about the weight that she'd carried in her heart for the past twenty-three years.

"Oh my God, Ashley," Savannah cried, the only one so far out of their group who had a child and could completely understand a parent's worst nightmare.

"Why didn't you ever say anything to us, to me?" Mia asked.

"It's hard. It's still hard to talk about. Guilt is a terrible thing." She sniffed, fighting back tears. "When I got this case I thought that maybe this was the chance that had eluded me and my family for years. I finally had the means and resources of doing what the police couldn't do years ago."

"Do you think that's why Jean selected you, because she knows?" Savannah asked, understanding all too well the reach and wealth of knowledge that Jean possessed.

Four pairs of eyes settled on Ashley.

"The thought did occur to me. It wouldn't surprise me one bit. But I didn't want to mention it to her if she didn't know."

"That's probably best," Traci said.

They sipped their drinks.

"So, other than mind-altering sex, how do you feel about Elliot?" Mia asked, breaking the silence.

Ashley offered a shadow of a smile. "I like him. I really do. Beneath the tough exterior and all the bluster, there's a decent, caring man. Someone that I want to get to know better." She paused for a moment and looked from one supportive face to another. "I want it to be more than great sex."

Mia squeezed her hand. "I don't want you to get your hopes up, Ash. From everything you've told us about Elliot he's not one to settle down. His job and the challenge of it have become his life. This may just be another assignment for him. You have to prepare yourself for that."

Ashley bobbed her head. "I know. But I'm

willing to see how far it will go before it's over. And I intend to make the most of every minute."

After the two-hour lunch they all decided to call it a day and promised to touch base with each other during the week. Ashley returned to the apartment and found it empty. She walked through the sprawling space touching the things they'd touched, breathing the air they'd breathed. She walked down the hall to her bedroom. She pushed open the door and her breath caught in her chest. On the nightstand was a crystal vase filled to overflowing with a burst of orange and peach colored roses. Propped up in front of the vase was a plain white envelope.

She crossed the room and lifted the envelope, turned it over and opened it. There was a card inside. The handwriting was even and strong.

"It was real. Don't doubt it. See you later. E."

She pressed the note to her chest, leaned down and inhaled the heady scent of the roses. She read the note again. Maybe her life had morphed into one of those sexy romance novels, where the inexplicable is commonplace. But every romance novel has a happily ever after ending. She placed the card on the table. She only wished she could flip the pages of this chapter of her life to the epilogue.

CHAPTER 15

At precisely six-thirty, Ashley and Elliot were seated in the front office of Happy Homes Adoption Agency. Elliot held Ashley's hand and the warmth and comfort of it was no pretense. She locked her fingers around his and easily slipped into her role as his loving wife.

"We at Happy Homes are very proud of our success record of pairing eligible parents with the perfect child," Gail Hastings, the case worker said. She looked over their application, nodding her head as she reviewed the information. She looked up at them. "Of course we'll have to verify everything and make several house visits. It's all part of our procedure."

"We totally understand," Elliot said. "All we want is the chance to be the great parents that I know we can be."

Ashley leaned forward, zeroed in on Gail. Her voice wobbled. "We've tried everything," she said. "In vitro didn't work and we began running out of money. We're down to our last hundred thousand dollars." She turned sad eyes on Elliot. "We can't risk going through the heartache and disappointment again. Adoption is our last chance." She lowered her head and covered her face with her hands.

Elliot put his arm around her shoulders and pulled her close. He mouthed, "I'm sorry," to Gail. She nodded her head in understanding.

"We'll certainly do everything we can, Mr. and Mrs. Morgan." She handed Ashley a tissue.

Ashley sniffed and wiped her eyes. "Thank you," she murmured.

"We have all of your information. We'll be in touch." She stood. The interview was over.

Elliot helped Ashley to her feet. He extended his hand to Gail. "Thank you for your time."

"Of course."

They turned to leave. Once they were outside, Elliot spun her around and kissed her fully on the lips. "You were damned good in there and the tears were a nice touch."

Ashley grinned. "I was kinda good, wasn't I?"

"Very. Let's go home and celebrate."

Curled up together on the couch, Ashley sipped on a glass of wine and Elliot worked on a bottle of beer as they watched video images from several windows on their computer. The images were from five of the locations they'd visited.

"Nothing out of the ordinary," Elliot said.

"What about audio?"

"I played the tapes earlier today. Nothing."

"Hopefully by tomorrow, we'll get a hit from the e-mail account."

She draped her legs across his lap. "This is like looking for a needle in a haystack. There are hundreds of agencies and who's to say that the ones on our list are even involved?" She tossed her head back against the cushion of the couch and closed her eyes.

"We're just getting started," he said. "We'll keep digging until we find what we're looking for." He leaned over and kissed her forehead. "We have two more to visit tomorrow." He took a last look at the recorded video then shut down the computer. "Patience," he added.

She opened her eyes and looked at him. "I've been patient for twenty-three years," she said softly. "I'm about out of patience."

Elliot stroked her cheek. She captured his hand and held it against her face. "Ready to turn in? It's after midnight."

"Your room or mine?" she asked.

"Let's do something wild and crazy." He rubbed her thigh.

She sat up. "Something more wild and crazy than what's been going on since we met?"

"Yeah, my room, two nights in a row!"

She laughed. "You're on."

"Last one in fixes breakfast," he said, leaping up from the couch and making a move for the hallway.

Ashley grabbed the tail of his shirt, throwing him off his stride and pushed past him. She took off down the hall with Elliot hot on her heels. She yelped and giggled as she burst through his door.

He grabbed her and tossed her on the bed, landing solidly down next to her. He rolled on top of her, smothering her laughter. "You cheated," he said, nibbling her neck.

"You got a head start."

"You know what they do to cheaters?"

"What?"

"They get exposed . . . for who they really

are," he said, as he began unbuttoning her blouse.

"I plead guilty," she murmured against his mouth. "Guilty as charged."

Over the course of the next three weeks, they worked tirelessly, going on interviews, filling out forms and watching videos. The Trojan that was planted on the computers at the agencies through e-mail transmission turned up nothing out of the ordinary. From everything they'd discovered so far, the agencies on the list were all above board.

In between being frustrated by their lack of progress, they explored the city together, sat up long into the night sharing stories of their youth, high school, college, movies and music that they loved and hated. They found out that their favorite movie of all time was *When a Stranger Calls.*

"I think I woke up the whole neighborhood with my screaming," Ashley admitted over her laughter. "When the babysitter found out that the murderer had been making calls from the attic right in her house, oh my goodness, I lost it."

"That part had everyone going. But the sequel got me," Elliot admitted. "When that nut painted himself as part of the wall and stepped out behind her . . ."

"Yes," she squealed, giving a little shiver. "That was over the top."

Elliot talked about the rough life he'd lived growing up in Baltimore, the losses he'd seen, the destruction. "I guess that's why I chose the life that I did. Danger was part of my makeup. Survival. You know."

"But do you ever get tired of it? I mean the never knowing."

He breathed heavily as he twirled a strand of her hair around his finger. "Most of the time I don't think about it. At least I try not to. It's a job, a job that keeps my mind from focusing on me. But sometimes I wake up in some strange hotel, in some strange city and I have to ask myself what the hell I'm doing."

She listened to the steady beat of his heart. "What answer do you come up with?"

"I'm still trying to find out," he said, his voice taking on a wistful tone. "Maybe one day I will."

As Ashley lay curled next to him, she wondered if she would be a part of his *maybe.*

"It's been more than a month," Ashley said as they drove to Justin's Restaurant for dinner.

The famed eatery owned by P. Diddy —

aka Puffy to old-school buffs — was noted for the good food, friendly service and being a frequent haunt of celebrities. Somehow, through Elliot's vast array of connections, he'd secured VIP passes to see a one-night-only private show by Whitney Houston. Since her return to the spotlight after nearly a ten-year hiatus she was the hottest ticket in town.

"I know. I was sure we would have found something by now. Even I'm beginning to get impatient."

"Maybe we've been looking in the wrong places?"

"Any ideas?"

"What about the hospitals? That's where they snatched my sister. Everyone knows that even with precautions, hospital security sucks, especially in urban and low-income areas."

"If we took on the hospitals, that would expand our search exponentially. We're talking hundreds of metropolitan hospitals and thousands of employees, not to mention patients and their guests."

"True." She blew out a long sigh, her small bubble of hope bursting in her ears.

Elliot stole a glance at Ashley and saw the disappointment that pinched the corners of the mouth he loved to kiss. He reached across the gearshift and grabbed her hand. "We'll map out a plan, starting with the most likely hospitals and work our way through them."

She turned to him.

"Your sister is out there somewhere. If we can find the source of the abductions, I believe it will lead us to your sister. Don't ask me how I know." His eyes creased in concentration. "It's just a gut feeling."

Ashley swallowed over the sudden knot in her throat. "Thank you," she whispered.

"Don't thank me yet. And don't go getting all teary on me, we have some partying to do tonight."

She sniffed and her expression brightened. "That we do."

When they arrived at Justin's they were met at the door by a tuxedoed security guard who checked their names off on the VIP list before handing them over to the hostess to seat them. The setting was straight out of *E! Hollywood.* A red carpet ran from the door to the center of the space. Multileveled seating gave the invited guests a good view from any location. The stage was set up on a center platform and Whitney's band was in place, warming up with mini renditions of some of her hits. Just a quick look around attested to the who's who that had come out to support "The Voice."

"I'm totally impressed," Ashley said, as Elliot helped her into her seat.

He kissed the back of her neck. "That was my secret plan all along."

Within moments a waitress came to take their drink and dinner orders. The show was scheduled to start in less than an hour and the feel of anticipation electrified the air. Even the *celebrati* were awed by the chance to see her up close and personal after such a long absence. What made it extra special was that it was not televised, there was no media, just friends and devoted fans.

Their drinks arrived first and just as Ashley was taking her first sip of her apple martini, she squinted into the muted lighting and swore she spotted Gail Hastings sitting on the far side of the room.

"Is that Gail, the case worker from Happy Homes?" she asked, trying not to point, but steering him in her direction with a lift of her chin. "Over there on the second tier."

Elliot turned halfway in his seat.

"She has on the mint-green dress."

Elliot stared a bit harder. "You're right, it is her."

"Guess she has friends in high places, too," she said half in jest, partly in curiosity.

"Hmm," Elliot murmured. The hair on the back of his neck began to tingle the way it did when he was within inches of his target.

They didn't have time to focus on it any longer. The lights dimmed, the MC came to the mic and introduced one of the greatest voices of her generation.

For the next hour the audience was mesmerized and transported as the diva took them from her early work, to everything in between, up to her latest album. Intermittently she would share a little anecdote about how she'd come to sing a song or the first time she sang it. And before anyone was ready to let her go, the show ended to a thunderous standing ovation.

"Oh my God, that was incredible," Ashley gushed. "I can't begin to thank you for this."

He winked at her. "I can think of a few things."

She swiped his arm. "Naughty boy."

"You spoil me." He took her hand and kissed the back of it.

"Hey, there she is."

Elliot still held her hand but turned in his seat. He pulled her up to her feet. "Get your purse."

She took her purse and let Elliot lead her over to the bar.

"Gail?" she said, dipping her head to the side.

Gail turned from the bar and the surprise on her face was camera-ready. "Oh . . . Mr. and Mrs. Morgan." She pressed her hand to her chest and looked around as if the answer to their sudden appearance was somewhere behind them. "What a pleasant surprise. Did you see the entire show?"

"Yes, we did. Pretty hard to get tickets," Elliot said. "You're one of the lucky ones."

A tall, silver-haired gentleman came to stand by Gail's side. He stuck out his hand. "Dr. Ettinger."

"Most people don't know we're married," Gail said softly, allowing Elliot and Ashley in on their secret. "It just makes things messy at work. You understand."

The bulb went off in Ashley's head. This was *the* Dr. Ettinger who actually owned and operated the agency. She'd run across his name and picture in the files.

"Of course," Elliot said and flashed a grin. "Your secret is safe with us."

"So you two are in the market for adoption," Ettinger said, looking from one to the other.

Ashley linked her arm through Elliot's. "Yes, Doctor, we certainly are. Talking with your wife . . . Gail really gave us a lot of hope."

"I know you two are eager," Gail said, "but I'm confident we'll find a baby for you."

"Yes, I'm sure we'll be able to help you," Dr. Ettinger added.

"Thank you, Doctor," Ashley said.

"Have they had their home visit yet, dear?" the doctor asked.

"No, they haven't."

"Well, why don't we at least get that ball rolling while we finish up the background check."

"Of course." Ashley turned to Elliot with excitement in her eyes. "We'd welcome a visit. It brings us closer to our dream."

"Good. You should be hearing from us this week," Gail said.

"Thank you so much," Ashley gushed.

"Of course. Our job is to bring good people together with beautiful children who need a home. Unfortunately, it often takes some time to find a good match," Dr. Ettinger said.

"We, uh, totally understand that this whole process can be . . . costly," Elliot said, "but we're willing to pay whatever is necessary to bring a healthy baby into our lives and make a home for him or her." He spoke directly to Dr. Ettinger.

He clasped Elliot's shoulder and patted him. "We won't even concern ourselves with that right now. Let's just get you two through the maze of paperwork and take it from there."

Elliot bobbed his head.

"We better get going, sweetheart," Gail said, "Jackson and Phyllis will be wondering what happened to us."

"We're meeting friends for a late drink," Dr. Ettinger offered by way of explanation.

"Sure. Good night. Thanks for talking with us. We don't want to hold you up." Elliot stuck out his hand and shook the doctor's and then Gail's hand.

"You should get a call this week about scheduling a home visit," Gail said as she turned to leave.

Elliot and Ashley watched them as they walked out, and neither could deny the unsettling feeling that Dr. and Mrs. Ettinger had left behind.

CHAPTER 16

"Jazz, I need you to do a full background search on a Dr. Thomas Ettinger," Elliot was saying into the phone as he looked over the brochure from Happy Homes Adoption Agency.

It was Jazz who'd designed the kits that the ladies used, that came complete with micro cameras disguised as lapel pins or magnetic disks, bubble bath that could knock out a horse, dusting power that was actually to lift fingerprints and a host of other necessary gadgets. In addition to which she was a master researcher and software developer. If there was any dirt under the fingernail of a subject, Jasmine could find it.

"Not a problem," she said, "I'll get on it. As soon as I have something I'll let you know."

"Oh, and Jazz, look, this is just between us, but I need you to take a look at a cold case . . ."

"So how is everything going between you and Elliot?" Mia asked as they prepared a PowerPoint presentation for a client.

Ashley smiled. "I wish I could complain but I can't."

"You actually sound happy."

She turned to Mia. "You know what . . . I am. For the first time in a very long while, I feel happy inside, Mia. I look forward to the end of the day, the nights, the mornings. We enjoy each other, in and out of the bed," she quickly added. "And as much as I hated to admit it, he's damned good at what he does and we work well together."

Mia nodded as she listened to her friend gush about her blossoming relationship, and dared to ask the question that sat in the room like a third person. "Are you falling in love with him, Ash?"

"I know it sounds silly and so romance novel cliché but I'm already in love with him. I've never felt this way about anyone before."

"And what about Elliot? Do you think he feels the same way?"

Ashley blew out a slow breath then looked at Mia. "I don't know."

Mia leaned forward on the desk and

linked her fingers together. "Ash, I know you're a big girl and you can take care of yourself in a street fight, but this is different. There are feelings involved. What are you going to do when this case is over and they send him off to who the hell knows where for months at a time? Are you prepared to deal with that?"

Ashley pushed back from the table and stood. She turned her back to Mia and slowly paced the floor. For a moment she glanced up at the ceiling as if the answer may be somewhere in the heavens. "It keeps me awake at night," she said, her voice distant and thin. "Sometimes I wake up in the morning with this paralyzing feeling that he's gone. And I can't move until I check every sound in the apartment, and hear his footsteps, or his off-beat humming, or the shower." She swallowed. "Just something to let me know that he hasn't left me, at least not yet." She turned and faced Mia. "But whatever happens I'll deal with."

"I know you will, sis." She waited a beat. "On another note, how is the case going — any leads?"

"We're not really sure but of all people to run into the other night . . ." She told Mia about their encounter with Gail and her husband Dr. Ettinger.

"It could be something or nothing at all. This is New York and you're liable to run into anyone. She could have been nervous for the reason that she said, most people don't know that they're married." She shrugged. "What's your gut telling you?"

"I can't put my finger on it. But their demeanor changed somehow during the course of the conversation."

"What do you mean?"

"They just all of a sudden wanted to bend over backward to accommodate us." She focused on Mia, trying to convey the sense of something awry to her.

"Could be that it eased an awkward situation or that they want you to help them keep their little secret if they help you."

"I suppose. One good thing came out of it all."

"What's that?"

"We got our appointment for a home visit. Tomorrow, 10:00 a.m."

Elliot and Ashley finished taking a last look around the apartment. Even though Ashley spent most nights in Elliot's bed, for the purposes of the visit they'd moved all of Ashley's belongings into Elliot's room leaving her room as the guest room or potential nursery.

The doorbell rang at precisely 10:00 a.m. Ashley looked to Elliot. "Ready?"

"Yes, dear," he teased, giving her rear a gentle love tap.

"Not in front of company," she said, leaning up to him and kissing him full on the lips. She used her thumb to wipe away the residue of her lip gloss.

Ashley buzzed the front door and watched on the lobby camera as a young man and woman approached the elevator.

"They're on their way up."

Moments later their front doorbell rang. Ashley and Elliot answered it together. The team introduced themselves as Wendy and Glen. They showed their identification along with a printout on Happy Homes letterhead indicating the appointment time and place.

They were young — in their late twenties to early thirties, very social-service-looking — serious about their work. They came complete with a checklist of questions, forms and a digital camera. While Elliot and Ashley filled out forms, Glen took photographs of the apartment.

"Is this where you plan to live?" Wendy asked, but it almost sounded like an accusation.

"Yes. Is that a problem?" Elliot asked.

"No." She made some notes. "Are you

200

planning to work, Mrs. Morgan, once you get the child?"

"No. My plan is to stay home and raise my baby." She looked to Elliot for confirmation and he nodded in agreement.

"I see," Wendy said, but clearly she didn't, as she sounded, once again, disturbed by their answers.

Glen returned to the living room. "All done," he announced. "You have a beautiful place."

"Thank you," Ashley said.

Wendy shot Glen a look of reproach. His pockmarked face reddened.

Wendy closed her leather folder with a snap and stood. "I think that covers everything." She reached into her wallet and took out a business card. "If you have questions, you can call. Thank you for your time."

"How long will the process be now that we've had a home visit?"

"Every case is different," she said noncommittally. "Good luck." She turned and walked toward the door with Glen trailing behind.

Elliot walked with them to the front door and let them out. "Thanks again," he said, shutting the door behind them. "Feel a little chilly in here to you?" he asked tongue in cheek.

"That is one cold sister," Ashley said. "Not a smile, not a kind word."

"No personality." He flopped down on the couch. "Can you imagine parents who are really looking to adopt and have to deal with her?"

Ashley shook her head. "After all we've been dealing with this past month and a half I almost feel like I am trying to adopt."

Elliot made a sound in his throat. "I know. Weird. I feel the same way."

Ashley curled her legs beneath her and adjusted her body in his direction. "You ever think you'll have kids of your own?" she asked and the instant the question was out of her mouth she wanted to snatch it back.

He clasped his hands behind his head and leaned back against the couch cushions. "The kind of life I lead, there's never been room in my life for kids, family, settling down. It just wouldn't be fair."

Yet he'd been willing to settle down once before, with Lynn, Ashley thought. But apparently not with her.

"Hey." She popped up from her seated position. "Wanna check out a movie tonight, if you don't have plans?" she asked to change the direction of the conversation. She didn't need him to see how his answer had affected her.

"Hmm, sure, why not. Doesn't that new Jamie Foxx movie start tonight."

"Yeah, I think it does." She swallowed over the burn in her throat. "I'll check." She walked off to the spare room where she'd kept her laptop. She sat down at the desk, covered her face and cried.

"Hey, Jazz," Elliot said, "hang on a sec, I'm driving. Let me pull over." He signaled and moved into the far-right lane and pulled to a stop in front of an outdoor café. "What do you have for me?"

"Not as much as I would like. I checked your Dr. Ettinger every which way but loose. Based on everything I've come up with he's a straight shooter. He's been running that clinic for just about ten years. Before that he was Chief of Staff at Methodist Hospital."

"Hmm, thanks, J."

"There is something else."

"What's that?"

"Prior to twenty years ago I can't find a scrap of anything on this guy. It's like he didn't exist."

"What?"

"I'm still checking but prior to 1984, the good doctor was a no-show."

Elliot frowned. "Keep checking, Jazz, and

keep me posted."

"I sure will."

He disconnected the call. *Who are you, Dr. Ettinger?*

When Elliot got back to the apartment later that evening, he walked in on a ringing phone. It wasn't quite six. He didn't expect Ashley back until much later. She and Mia had a dinner meeting with a client. He tossed his jacket on the couch and walked into the kitchen, snatching up the phone on the fourth ring.

"Morgan residence," he said, and kind of liked the sound of it.

"Mr. Morgan?"

"Yes. Who is this?" He glanced at the caller ID and it showed Anonymous.

The caller cleared her throat. "It's Gail, from the adoption agency."

He pulled out his PDA from his jacket pocket, connected the USB cord to the phone and pressed record. "Oh, hello. How are you?" He looked at the dial on his PDA and saw that it was recording. "Do you have news for us?"

"I may have a child for you and your wife."

"That's wonderful! This is the news we've been praying for," he said, bursting with feigned enthusiasm.

She cleared her throat again. "I was hoping that we could meet, privately, away from the office."

Bingo. Elliot felt the adrenaline rush through his veins. "Uh, a private meeting?"

"With you and your wife, of course."

"Of course. When did you want to meet?"

"Tomorrow evening. Eight o'clock at Bombay on East Seventy-second Street and Riverside Drive."

"I know the place."

"Good. I'll make reservations and see you and your wife at eight."

"Thank you. Thank you so much."

"Good night, Mr. Morgan."

"Good night."

The call disconnected and he turned off the recorder. This was it. He could feel it in every fiber of his being. Gail was going to make an offer, and once she did the trail had to lead back to the real source. He was hard-pressed to think that Gail Hastings was at the top of this particular food chain. No. It was someone else. That much he was sure of.

He was itching to share the news with Ashley and couldn't wait for her to get home. *Home.* His stomach jumped. He hadn't thought of anyplace as home in more than too many years.

Elliot pulled open the fridge and took out a bottle of Coors. What would it be like not to be in a pretend relationship with Ashley Temple, but in a real one? He twisted off the top and took a long, icy-cold swallow.

After their awkward and tense beginnings, they'd found a rhythm together, and not just in bed, that was an added plus. They found their rhythm in day-to-day life, doing for each other, looking out for each other, listening, supporting, laughing with each other.

He enjoyed her company. He looked forward to seeing her standing at the stove in the morning, and inhaling the scent of her shower gel at night. Over the weeks that they'd shared a life as a husband and wife, he'd come to embrace the idea of Ashley in his life, enjoying it. And it had become so easy and comfortable that it felt, natural, the way it should be.

When he thought of Ashley, it made him smile from the inside out, from her no-nonsense attitude to her unbelievable sensuality. She was smart, beautiful, funny, sexy and a damned good agent.

He sat down on the recliner, pressed the button on the arm that raised the leg rest.

And for all that was good and wonderful about the life he was living, he knew that it was temporary. They were actors in a play and soon they'd get their curtain call. If things moved in the direction he felt that they would, that call may come much sooner rather than later. Then he and Ashley would go back to the way it was before.

Something deep inside him twisted and he felt an emptiness inside. And he realized with sudden clarity that he didn't want "the way it was before." That realization scared him, scared him more than flying bullets, car bombs and threats of terrorism. Because he had no gadget, no protective gear, no retaliation to fight off feelings. He'd tried and for a long time he'd been successful. Until Ashley.

Elliot finished off his beer. He could almost see himself with Ashley for the long haul. But that wouldn't be fair to her. And he had no idea what he would do for a living if he stopped his line of work.

Humph, wishful thinking. He was certain that making a life with him was the last thing on Ashley's mind.

He felt the vibration of his cell phone inside his pants pocket. He pulled it out and checked the lighted screen. It was a text from Jasmine. *May have a line on that* other *project. Need to unravel some threads and let you know.* He halfway smiled. At least when he left her for good, he hoped to leave Ashley with some answers.

CHAPTER 17

When Ashley came in later that evening she was bubbling with excitement over the latest client that MT Management had landed, which was a new cable station that wanted to sponsor a virtual watch party of its launch in all of its markets across the country.

"It's an incredible opportunity," she enthused as she stepped out of her shoes and tucked them away in the closet that she and Elliot now shared. She pulled her hair away from her face with a headband that had magically appeared.

For a moment, Elliot was taken aback by her raw, natural beauty. Never one to wear makeup, her warm brown complexion was clear and glowed with vitality. Her large, luminous brown eyes sparkled with energy when she talked in concert with her slender fingers that fluttered and flowed, organizing the distribution of her narrative like a symphony conductor. Her body was a work of art and her smile could warm the coldest room. He was totally enchanted with her, thrilled by her, turned on by her and very much in love with her.

"So what do you think?" she asked, diving onto the bed and landing next to him, unceremoniously jolting him from his assessment of her.

His eyes danced over her for a moment. He stroked the curve of her jaw. "I think that there's not a better team out there that can do what you and Mia do. And they're damned lucky to get you," he said, searching every corner of his mind to piece together what she'd been talking about while he was daydreaming.

She rolled onto her back and giggled like a little girl. "MT Management is seriously in the big league. The sky is the limit."

Elliot braced himself on his elbow, leaned down and kissed her ever so tenderly. "Congratulations."

The rhythm of Ashley's breathing stuttered then sped up as she witnessed an outright look of lust in his eyes.

Elliot kissed her again while he lifted her top. "I want to make love to you," he said against the swell of her breasts, his voice laden with an emotion that he couldn't name. He could never tell her how he felt, what he was feeling about her. It wasn't fair. But he could show her. He could show her by the way he touched her, the way he kissed her lips, the way he got her wet enough to receive all of him, the way he moved inside her and held her on the brink until she could no longer bear the denial. Those things he could do. But he could never tell her what it all meant.

They lay together afterward beneath the soft light of the full moon. The evenings had grown warmer and the days longer as spring began to step aside for summer.

Elliot held her close, gently running his hand along the soft curve of her spine. "Got a call today."

"From who?" she asked, her voice heavy with sleep.

"Gail Hastings. She wants to meet us, privately."

Ashley blinked away her fatigue. She was fully awake now. She pushed herself into a semi-sitting position. "When did she call?"

"Earlier this evening."

"Why didn't you tell me?"

"I'd intended to but I got so caught up in your coup today and then . . ." He ran his thumb across her still-tender nipples. "You know I get distracted," he joked.

She swiped at his hand. "This is important."

He sat up. The sheet slid down to his
waist. "I'm sorry. I know. This may be the
break we've been waiting for. She sounded
like she wants to make some kind of deal.
We'll have to go the meeting and just play it
by ear."

Ashley was bobbing her head in the semi-
darkness. Her mind went fast-forward to
finally cracking the case and finding out
who was behind the abductions, and somewhere at the end of that rainbow she would
find her sister.

"Her birthday is in two weeks," she said
softly. "She would be twenty-three."

Elliot drew her close. She rested her head
on his chest. "If Layla is out there, we'll
find her. I promise you."

They went over all the details one more
time before they headed out. Ashley would
ask all the questions and Elliot would speak
for both of them. They had to be sure to
insist that money was no object. They had
money and could get more.

Ashley had a mini recorder that looked
like a cell phone inside her purse that she
would activate as soon as conversation

began. The digital device could record up to five hours before you had to upload the audio files to a computer.

"Ready?" Elliot asked.

Ashley angled her head and put her hand on her hip. "I'm supposed to be asking all the questions," she joked.

"Yes, dear," he tossed back. He put his arm around her waist. "Let's go."

The Bombay Lounge was a high-end, very expensive restaurant complete with authentic Indian food and decor located in the posh Upper East Side of Manhattan.

Ashley and Elliot arrived minutes before eight and were seated right away. Gail Hastings had already arrived. And so had Dr. Ettinger.

Elliot and Ashley, hand-in-hand, greeted Gail and the doctor and sat down at the round table.

"I'm so glad you could come," Gail began.

"Yes, we feel very confident that we can help you," Dr. Ettinger stated.

Ashley grabbed Elliot's hand and squeezed it. "You found a baby for us?" Her eyes widened with hope.

The answer was interrupted by the waiter who came to take their order. Dr. Ettinger

213

made some recommendations to Ashley and Elliot.

"We think we may have found the perfect baby for you," Gail said once the waiter was gone.

Ashley's hands flew to her mouth. Her eyes filled with emotion.

"We've gone over your entire profile, did a check on your backgrounds and we have every reason to believe that you will make ideal parents," Dr. Ettinger said.

Elliot used the opportunity to kiss Ashley. He turned to Gail and her husband. "I told Ash that we finally found the right place when we came to you."

"So what's the next step?" Ashley asked.

"I'm sure you're both aware that adoptions can generally take up to a year," Gail said, playing out each word.

Elliot straightened in his seat. "But I thought you said you had a baby for us."

Dr. Ettinger held up his hand. "What my wife is saying is that for very select couples, couples that are needy and deserving . . . Well, sometimes we can speed things up."

Ashley ran her tongue across her lips. Her voice lowered. "So what do we need to do . . . to help?"

"Speed is often costly," Dr. Ettinger stated.

Ashley looked at Elliot.

"I can't impress upon you enough that for us money is no object," Elliot said. "Whatever it takes."

The waiter brought their drinks and the food was right behind it.

Elliot was coiled as tight as a cobra ready to strike. It took all of his training and strength of will not to reach across the table, snatch the both of them by the necks and shake all the answers out of them. Instead he concentrated on his meal, making small talk and sipping his drink.

When the dishes had been cleared away, Gail and Dr. Ettinger resumed the conversation as if discussing selling babies during dinner was bad manners.

"I won't beat around the bush. If you are truly interested, it will cost you $50,000 now and $50,000 upon delivery."

"How long is delivery going to take?" Ashley asked.

"No more than two weeks. Maybe sooner," Gail answered.

Ashley expelled a breath of relief. "Two weeks," she said, her voice shaky with excitement. "We've waited so long." Tears slid down her cheeks. She grabbed the white-linen napkin and dabbed at her eyes. "Sorry," she murmured. "Our dream is so close." She turned to Elliot. "Oh, honey . . ."

"You said $50,000. How do we work that out?" Elliot asked.

"We'll be in touch when we're sure about the baby. At that time we'll arrange to get the deposit. When we bring the baby we'll expect the balance. You'll be given all the papers to make it official."

The waiter reappeared with the check. Elliot went to take out his wallet.

"No, please, Mr. Morgan," Dr. Ettinger said. He put a black American Express card in the leather folder and handed it to the waiter.

"Can we drop you somewhere?" Gail asked.

"No, thank you — we drove," Elliot answered.

"When do you think we can expect to hear from you?" Ashley asked.

"Soon, I promise," Gail said, reaching across the table to cover Ashley's hand with her own.

Ashley nodded her head.

On the ride home Ashley and Elliot tossed kudos back and forth for their performances.

"You were totally on point with the questions. All of their responses will be used to nail them," Elliot said.

"You weren't so bad yourself, handsome." She squeezed his thigh. "The strong, take-charge husband. Perfect role for you."

He gave a mock bow as he pulled to a stop at the red light. "But I have to give it to you, Ash, the tears again were a real nice touch. How do you manage to cry on cue like that?"

Her brows flicked for a moment. "When I think about my parents and what they went through, how I felt . . . I imagine the pain that some other family will go through to make our dreams come true. Was Layla some desperate family's dream come true?" Her voice cracked. She lowered her head. "I'm sorry."

"You have no reason to apologize. It was insensitive of me." He took a quick glance at her. "I think we're finally on track. This may all be over soon, and hopefully we'll make a lot of families happy, including yours."

"And what about those families that will have to give up children they've grown to love and the children who love them?"

Elliot was silent. He had no answer.

The following morning they met with Jean and Bernard at The Cartel headquarters.

"Based on the information that you've provided, we're putting Dr. Ettinger and his wife under twenty-four hour surveillance," Jean said. "They could very well be getting these babies from mothers who are willingly giving them up for the right price. Either way, we'll get to the bottom of it."

"Any luck with the rest of the list?" Bernard asked.

Ashley shook her head. "Clean."

Jean nodded her head. "So for now, Happy Homes is our target." She closed the file on the desk. "Keep us posted."

Ashley and Elliot rose.

"Seems you two are getting along much better," Jean said, as she adjusted several stacks of paper on her desk.

Her comment froze them in place. They weren't sure if they should respond or ignore her.

Jean slipped her red-rimmed glasses from her nose. "Have a good day."

They practically ran out of the door.

"It's spooky how she knows things," Ashley whispered as they hurried out.

"Yeah, creepy. Her sixth sense is legendary," Elliot said, as they rounded the last flight of stairs onto the ground floor.

Jasmine was coming up from the basement as they walked to the front door.

"Hey, E, Ashley."

They turned to the sound of their names.

"Jazz," they said in unison.

"I'm glad I ran into you guys. I have some information on your case. I was going to take it up to Jean."

"What do you have?"

She handed over the file. "I'm almost 90 percent sure that Dr. Ettinger and Dr. Lester are the same person."

CHAPTER 18

Ashley and Elliot spent the rest of the afternoon going over every line of information that Jasmine had put together.

"When you put their files side by side they're practically identical," Elliot said, "from city of birth to professions. I mean there are a few variations, but nothing major."

"They can't be the same person, they look nothing alike."

"Nothing that a little nip and tuck couldn't cure. Same body types, complexion . . ." He turned to Ashley. "What's wrong?" he asked, seeing the strained look on her face.

"I don't know," she said, her voice drifting off. "Something is nagging me, but I can't put my finger on it."

Elliot gently massaged the back of Ashley's neck and she moaned in pleasure. "Put it out of your head for a while and it will come to you."

She closed her eyes and let Elliot's fingers loosen the tension in her body. "You're probably right. I'm overthinking this."

"Exactly. I'm going to take a hot shower and then check the videos. From the other locations."

"Do you think we should still pursue a hospital connection?" Ashley asked, stretching.

"Let's see what happens with Gail and the good doctor."

As Ashley lay in bed, all of the details that they'd been given by Jasmine ran around in disarray in her head. She was a person of detail and order, much like Mia. She firmly believed that for every endeavor there had to be a plan for a successful outcome.

She listened to Elliot's deep, even breathing and let it relax her and allow her mind to clear of all the stuff that was cluttering it and blocking what she needed to see.

One by one, she took the information that she had and lined it up like index cards on the white board of her mind: names, years, profession, affiliations, hospitals. Dr. Ettinger. Dr. Lester. Concentrate. What was she missing? The answer hung on the fringes of her consciousness. Her mother. Layla.

She moved the cards around in her head.

Her stomach suddenly tensed. She jerked up in bed. Her heart hammered. Could it be? She eased out of bed and tiptoed to the front. Digging in her purse that she'd left on the couch, she took out her cell phone.

It was nearly 2:00 a.m. but her dad was a notorious insomniac. He'd be annoyed by the call, but he'd be awake. Her father picked up the phone on the first ring.

"Dad, it's Ashley."

"I guess it is. You're the only one to call me Dad."

"Dad, listen, I need you to try to remember something. Was Dr. Herman Lester the name of Mom's first doctor before she went to the specialist?"

"Hell, girl, I don't know. That was more than twenty years ago."

"Dad, I know. But please, think. It's important."

"Is this about Layla?" His voice rose in anxiety. "Is that what this is about? Why are you asking questions about that at this time? Why? You know how it upsets your mother."

Her heart started to break all over again when she heard the anguish in her father's voice. Her mother may have had the break-down, but her dad suffered in many other ways. Not only had he lost a child, he'd lost the woman that he married.

"Dad, please. I'm sorry. I'm sorry. Look, we'll talk another time. Get some rest." She waited for him to say something and when he didn't she said good-night.

Totally shaken, she sat down on the couch, drew her knees to her chest and lowered her head. She wasn't sure how long she sat there, drifting in and out of sleep until the chirping of her cell phone snapped her fully awake. She shook her head to clear it. Calls this time of the night were never about good news, some part of her brain surmised. She snatched up the phone from the couch and frowned when she saw the number. She pressed Talk.

"Dad? Is something wrong? Is it Mom?"

"I went through the old bills and notes," he began. "I found one from a Dr. Lester."

Ashley's heart banged in her chest. "Is the first name Herman?"

"Just says Dr. H. Lester, Winston Medical Center. That's where your mother went . . . in the beginning. To the clinic."

Ashley's throat had tightened. She remembered going with her mother on her visits when she was first pregnant with Layla. She remembered sitting in the waiting room, looking at magazines with chubby-cheeked babies on the cover and women all around her in varying stages of pregnancy. But then her mother couldn't see Dr. Lester anymore, yes, that was his name, because her mother was high-risk.

Ashley could barely talk. "Thank you, Dad," she managed. "Please don't put that away. I may need it."

They said their goodbyes. Ashley's mind was on overdrive. The final piece of the puzzle was just out of her reach, but she knew she'd find it. She'd figure it out.

She walked back into the bedroom and sat down next to Elliot. He stirred, opened his eyes and squinted up at her.

"What're you doing up? What time is it?"

"Dr. Lester treated my mother."

He rubbed his eyes and sat up in the bed. "What? How do you know?"

"That's what was bugging me, the name. In the back of my mind. I couldn't figure how or why I thought I knew it." She went on to explain that she'd called her father and he'd found the bill from Dr. H. Lester.

"I don't remember seeing Winston Medical Center in the intel that we have."

"It wasn't. I know if I'd seen it I would have made the connection sooner."

"We'll get this info to Jazz in the morning and have her do a trace." He looked at her with a new admiration. "Have you been to

224

sleep at all?"

"No." She breathed heavily and rested her head on his chest. He wrapped his arms around her and drew her close. "Try to get some rest."

"Some super spy you turned out to be," she teased, poking him lightly in the side. "You didn't even budge when I was tiptoeing around in here. I could have been an intruder."

"I figured I had a kick-ass Cartel sister in my bed who would make sure I was safe and sound," he said, nibbling on her neck.

She laughed and rolled on top of him to let him know just what a Cartel sister was capable of.

Elliot hung up the phone just as Ashley emerged from the bathroom wrapped from head to toe in towels.

"I just got off with Jasmine. She said she should have something for us in a couple of hours. I've been going over the video and the e-mails from all of the locations, including Happy Homes. There's nothing. Not a letter out of place. If there is anything going down, it's not happening at these locations."

"So what are you thinking?"

"If Gail and her husband are brokering babies they're doing it from someplace else, another office, their home . . . I don't know."

"I'm sure you're right, and it's obvious that whatever they're doing is shaky. Why not have us meet at the agency? Why take us to someplace private if everything was aboveboard?"

"Exactly." He ran his hand over the morning stubble on his chin and jaw. His cell phone rang beside him. He looked at the dial. It read Restricted. "Hello?"

"Mr. Morgan?"

"Yes, who is this?"

"This is Gail. I wanted to let you know that based on what we discussed we'd need the first part by the end of this week. Things are moving along much more quickly than we expected."

He stole a look at Ashley and mouthed, "Gail. Uh, is tomorrow okay?"

"Of course. I'll be in touch with the arrangements." The call was disconnected.

Elliot dropped the phone onto the couch. "I need to get over to see Jean. We're going to need the first fifty grand by tomorrow."

"Give me fifteen minutes and I'll go with you."

He pulled her unceremoniously down onto his lap. "Don't you have a real job? Somebody has to work to pay the bills around here," he teased, while wiggling his way under her towel.

She hopped up and snaked out of his grasp. "I actually do need to go into the office. We have tons of work to do with this new cable station account. Although, I'm sure Mia would understand if I came in later."

"Go on to the office. I'm not gonna run off with the loot like in the movies," he joked.

"Very funny. Okay. I guess you're right, and I don't want to leave Mia in the lurch." She started to walk off then looked back at him over her shoulder. "If you need me . . . just put your lips together and blow."

"Lauren Bacall ain't got nothing on you, baby," he chuckled.

She sashayed away to the rhythm of his whistling some unrecognizable tune.

"You'll be wearing a wire," Bernard was saying as he stacked the money into a plain black leather bag. "And we'll have some agents stationed nearby for surveillance."

"Women are so much more unobtrusive. We'll use Savannah and Danielle if necessary," Jean said.

"Not a problem," Bernard agreed, zipping up the bag. He handed it to Elliot. "You've done this a million times. You know the drill."

Elliot took the bag. "Walk in the park."

Gail had arranged to stop by Elliot and Ashley's apartment to pick up the money and drop off some paperwork.

"They're very cautious," Elliot was saying to Ashley as he hooked up a video camera above a piece of artwork in the living room. There were bugs all over the apartment to pick up even whispered conversation. But Elliot had a feeling that this exchange was going to be short and sweet. "They're not bringing us anywhere that can connect them to anything out of the ordinary. Coming here was an especially nice touch." He hopped down off the step stool and stood back to admire his handiwork. "Perfect."

"They should be here any minute," Ashley said.

"Yeah." He stepped up to her and wrapped his arm around her waist before swooping down for a quick kiss. "Ready?"

"Hmmm, hmm," she said against his lips and she had a sudden flash of what life would be like for her when this was over. How empty it would be. Suddenly she clung to him, surprising them both.

"What is it?" he asked, turning her face

up to look at him.

She shook her head. "We're close," she said, instead of what was on her mind, the fact that this playacting they'd been doing had become real for her and how she was desperately, deeply in love with him, and she didn't know what she was going to do when he was no longer in her life. But of course she could never say that. They were adults, playing house and enjoying each other's company. No more. No less. He'd made it clear that his life was his job, a job that could take him to the ends of the earth at any given time for months on end. "This will all be over soon," she added, the double entendre having a special significance for her.

Elliot inhaled deeply and pressed her close to his chest. Yes, it will, he thought.

At nine o'clock Gail Hastings walked through their door. She'd come alone, which Elliot found significant. If anything were to go down, Gail would take the fall. He'd love to be a fly on the wall in their marriage. By nine-fifteen they had what appeared to be official documents and Gail was gone with the cash.

"The clock is now ticking," Elliot said as he locked the door behind her.

CHAPTER 19

"Elliot, it's Jasmine. I have some info on that side case that you asked me about," the message said. "I'm going to send the data to your PDA. Any questions, give me a call. Sorry it took so long. Seemed to be a rush on spying this week," she joked.

Elliot grinned. She must have called while they were making the exchange with Gail. While Ashley was on the phone in the bedroom with Mia, he went into the kitchen and booted up his PDA. Adrenaline rushed through his veins as he read the information. The overwhelming urge to kick down Gail and her husband's door had him shaking with rage, and he didn't want to rip up the seeds of hope that would never materialize because of something stupid that he did. He knew he had to keep himself in check. Overreaction could blow everything. This had to be done the right way down to the letter. But at some point he knew he was going to scramble the alphabet.

The next two weeks were like hell. The waiting was unbearable. They were so close to breaking the case wide open but it all hinged on that last phone call, the last meeting. The ball was in the other team's court.

And then the call came. They had a little girl. Three days old. They would bring the baby within the hour.

"They're playing this real close," Elliot said. "They're trying like hell to make sure that no one but them has time to make any moves."

"I'll call Bernard," Ashley said, shifting into action. "He needs to get someone here before they arrive." She was relieved when Bernard picked up on the second ring.

"Putting someone in the house at this point is too risky. They could easily run into each other in the lobby. Elliot is fully authorized to make an arrest. You keep the baby safe and Elliot can take care of the rest. We'll get social services over there as soon as Elliot throws on the cuffs."

Ashley hung up the phone. "Looks like we're on our own." She ran down to him what Bernard had said.

"Makes sense. You cool with this?"

She nodded.

"Good."

Elliot went into the bedroom and retrieved his gun from the top of the closet, checked the safety and tucked it into his waistband at the base of his spine then got his badge, which he hung around his neck, beneath his shirt.

Ashley watched his precision movements from the doorway, the cold, almost-calculated look that descended across his features, the way his eyes darkened and his body tensed. This was who he was, what he did. There was a dangerous energy that radiated from him. And when he turned his head in her direction, she didn't recognize him. Her heart thundered. And then he smiled.

"They should be here any minute."

"Yes," she said, her voice barely above a whisper.

"Come on." He walked over to her, draped his arm around her shoulder. "Let's go sit down and pretend to be a happily married couple and snag these bastards."

They were seated at the kitchen table when the lobby bell rang. Elliot pushed back from the table. He went to the intercom, saw that it was Gail and the good doctor on the lobby cameras. He buzzed them in. He turned to Ashley as he removed his gun and checked it one last time.

Ashley swallowed. "Let's do this."

He leaned over and kissed her forehead. "It's gonna go down smooth as silk."

The front doorbell rang. Ashley opened it. Gail walked in first with her husband behind her. She was carrying a large tote bag with a flat bottom. She walked past them and gently placed the bag down on the couch. She reached down inside and took out the newborn baby girl wrapped in pink. She stood there with the baby in her arms.

"Do you have the money?" Dr. Ettinger asked.

Elliot went to the table and brought back the bag that held the balance of the hundred thousand dollars.

"Fifty thousand, just like you asked," he said.

Dr. Ettinger went to the bag and opened it. He lifted several packs of wrapped bills and flipped through them. He turned to his wife and lifted his chin. Gail handed the baby to Ashley. Dr. Ettinger zipped up the bag.

"Our business is concluded. I'm sure you will be very happy."

"But you won't," Elliot said, pulling his weapon. "FBI. You're under arrest."

Gail screamed. Ashley clutched the baby.

Bernard and another agent burst through the door, grabbed the doctor and Gail, pinning them to the wall as they were read their rights. They'd been listening to everything from the microphone bud that they had in their ears. And while the Ettingers were busy selling a baby, the FBI was searching their apartment in Manhattan and their house on Long Island.

By the time the apartment was cleared and social services had come to take the baby, which they were told had been taken from Long Shore Hospital, Ashley was physically shaken.

"I need to go out for a while," Elliot said. "Some things I need to take care of. You gonna be okay?"

She felt numb. She nodded.

He looked at her for a long moment. "See you in a few hours."

Left alone, Ashley was tormented by the enormity of the past few hours, the past month. How could Gail and her husband live with themselves after what they'd done? She couldn't begin to imagine what would crawl out from beneath their rug once it was fully pulled. And for right now, she wouldn't. She curled up into a ball on the couch and cried.

■ ■ ■ ■

Elliot worked with the search team for hours. By the time they were done they'd secured computers, files and journals. He was still sitting at the conference table at New York's FBI headquarters when Bernard came in bearing coffee.

"It's pretty clear that this Robert Ettinger is the mastermind behind a nationwide baby-selling ring. The bureau is lining up indictments for folks all over the city. You should be damned proud of yourself."

Elliot raised bleary eyes in Bernard's direction and briefly wondered how Bernard had managed to stay so pressed and unruffled after the night they'd had.

"Yeah," he said, the one word a testament to his exhaustion and his dilemma. He opened a file, compiled from information taken from the Ettinger house and what Jasmine had put together at his request, turned it around and showed it to Bernard.

Bernard slipped on his half-framed glasses, the only indicator of his age, and sat down. After several long moments, he slowly removed his glasses and set them beside the folder. "What are you going to do?"

CHAPTER 20

When Elliot dragged himself back to the apartment, it was eerily quiet. He walked through the rooms to his bedroom and immediately knew that something was wrong. All of Ashley's things were gone. He quickly retraced his steps and went down the hall to the other side of the apartment. He pushed open Ashley's door. Empty.

He felt as if he'd been kicked in the gut. The force of the realization that she was actually gone was so strong that it was physical. He turned in a slow circle, momentarily lost and off center. He gazed down at the file in his hand. Exhaustion gripped him one final time. He lowered himself onto the bed, supine, threw his arm across his eyes and begged for sleep.

Savannah, Danielle and Mia helped Ashley with the last of her things.

For Ashley, the decision to leave the apartment and Elliot was more difficult than anything she'd ever done. Her insides felt raw as if they'd been gouged out with some sharp object. Her head pounded and she was sure that her heart was broken. But what choice did she have? It was better to leave now than to watch him walk away from her. That, she knew she would not be able to bear.

"You should have at least left him a note," Savannah was saying as she unzipped one of the suitcases.

"I don't know why you left at all," Danielle added. "You know you love the man, just work it out."

"It's not that simple, Dani. I can't just profess my love for a man who would just as soon hop on a plane to the jungles of the rain forest as make love to me."

Mia put her hands on her hips. "I have to agree, Ash. You won't know what's on the man's mind until you lay your cards on the table."

"You can't be any more hurt than you are now if he doesn't give you the answers you want to hear. But if you don't pose the questions you'll never know."

Ashley plopped down on the side of her bed and looked up into the three concerned faces of her girls. Deep inside she knew they were right. But she didn't think she could stand to hear him actually say that he didn't want to be with her.

"I can't deal with this right now," she finally said. "I need some sleep." She slowly stood and gathered the trio in her arms, kissing each cheek. "Thank you guys for everything. Ya'll don't have to go home, but you gotta leave here. I'm beat."

Mia snatched up her purse in mock indignation. "I've been kicked out of better places than this."

"No, you haven't," Danielle said, pushing her toward the door.

"Call me if you need to talk," Savannah whispered and finger-waved on her way out.

Ashley sunk back across the bed and in moments she'd drifted off into a troubled sleep.

The sound of ringing and banging permeated her dreams. She'd been running, pushing through a series of never-ending doors in search of the answers that would lead her to what happened to her sister twenty-three years ago. At first she imagined that the noise was the sound of the doors slamming shut behind her and her ringing bells to gain entry to the empty rooms. But it wasn't her dream.

Groaning, she blinked against the darkness and pulled herself up. She peered at the digital clock. It was after ten. She'd been asleep all day. Struggling, she got up and went to the door.

"Who is it?"

"Elliot. I need to talk to you."

Elliot! She looked down at what she had on; baggy, dingy sweatpants and a wrinkled T-shirt. Her hair felt like it was matted down on one side and she could feel the crust in her eyes.

"Come on, Ash. Open the door."

She wiped her eyes and ran her fingers through her hair. Reluctantly she pulled the door open and stood in the frame, blocking him from entering.

"Trust me, you don't look *that* bad," he said, hoping to tease a smile out of her.

The instant she opened the door, his whole world shifted. There was suddenly daylight in the midst of his darkness. He felt a surge of possibility and an overwhelming desire to take her in his arms and never let her go. But of course he couldn't do that. The simple reality of her being back in her own apartment spoke volumes about everything. The case was over and so were they. That truth devastated him. But if this was what she wanted . . . He forced a smile.

She made a face and stepped aside. "What are you doing here?" she asked, walking behind him into her dual-purpose living and dining room.

"I have something you need to see. For the past couple of weeks, I've been feeding details to Jasmine."

Her heart began to race.

"Between what she found and what was pulled from the Ettinger's home, I've been working on putting this together all night and most of the day."

"Working . . . on what?"

He went into the inside jacket pocket of his FBI windbreaker and took out a rolled-up manila folder. He handed it to her. Her hand trembled as she reached out to take it.

Some time later she gazed up at him, her eyes teary from emotion and fatigue. "Do you think it's true?"

"I'm pretty sure," he said, nodding his head.

The tears fell freely now. "So, what do we do?" she asked, her voice breaking like a scratched CD.

"You need to decide what you want to do with the information, Ash . . ." He paused and sat down beside her. "Whatever you decide, I'll support you. I promise you that."

Ashley broke down and sobbed. He gathered her in his arms and held her, letting her release all the years of hurt, and guilt and loss. He knew that whatever decision she made it would change lives for better or worse.

CHAPTER 21

The campus of Brooklyn College was in full swing as students rushed from one building to the next and geared up for the Homecoming Weekend. Located in Brooklyn's Midwood section, the sprawling campus was one of the borough's crown jewels. They walked toward the graduate buildings and the President's office.

It had been ages since she'd walked the halls of a college campus, Ashley thought as she and Elliot navigated their way to the administrative offices. The closest she'd come to being back in school was on her last assignment where she posed as a high school student.

"Should be around the next corner," Elliot said, referring to the college president's office.

Ashley's heart thumbed in anticipation. She'd spent two weeks of sleepless nights debating about what was the right thing to do. It had been a painful, but thoughtful decision. She only hoped it was the right one. And during that two weeks when she'd wrestled with what to do, Elliot was there to support her, just like he'd promised.

Elliot opened the door to the outer office, and they stepped into the reception area.

An auburn-haired receptionist greeted them. "President Stevenson is waiting for you. You can go right in."

Elliot tapped lightly on the door and they walked into President Stevenson's office. The elegant gentleman, surrounded by plaques and degrees, was seated behind an enormous cherrywood desk. The young woman, seated in front of his desk turned to look at them when they walked in, and Ashley's heart nearly stopped. They were her mother's eyes, wide and almost see-through brown. Her knees wobbled and Elliot held her tight around her waist. The birthmark, a dark circle the size of a quarter, rested by her right ear, which she didn't bother to hide with her hair. She remembered asking her mother if the mark would go away. Her mother had hugged her and told her no, saying that birthmarks were little touches from God as He sent each of us out into the world.

President Stevenson rose from his plush

high-backed leather seat. He extended his hand to Ashley and Elliot. "Please, have a seat." He waited for them to get settled. "Ms. Temple, Mr. Morgan this is Simone McDonald. Simone, these are the people that I told you about." He cleared his throat. "My secretary can get you anything you need. I have a meeting." He walked past Simone and squeezed her shoulder before walking out and closing the door softly behind them.

After several awkward moments of silence, Ashley angled her chair toward Simone.

"You don't know me from the man in the moon," Ashley began, speaking softly and deliberately. She looked Simone directly in her eyes. "But I know you."

Over the next hour, Ashley held Simone's hand as she told her about the months leading up to her birth, her arrival and the agony when she disappeared. She told her about the toll that it took on their parents and on her.

"We've never forgotten you," Ashley said as she wiped away Simone's tears and then her own. "Never stopped wanting to find you and believing that you were out there somewhere."

"What's my real name?" Simone finally asked.

"Layla. Your name is Layla."

Bernard, Ashley, Jasmine, Jean and Elliot were gathered in Jean's office a week later for a debriefing.

"According to all the documents that have been confiscated there are more than eight hundred children that have been abducted by this network alone over the past twenty years," Jean said, the disgust that she felt evident in her tone. "I hope those S.O.B.s rot in jail. The devastation they've caused is incalculable. Unraveling this mess is going to take a while. And reconnecting the stolen children with their biological families . . . that is an even bigger nightmare." She took a long breath. "But the birth families deserve to know, they deserve some closure." She turned to Ashley. "How is Layla handling the news?"

"The DNA results came back." She turned to Elliot and smiled. He'd worked magic to push it through quickly. "She's definitely my sister. She wants to meet our parents. She's pretty much taken care of herself since she was eighteen. Her adoptive parents divorced when she was twelve and her mother died four years ago. Our road will be rough but certainly not as rough as other families. I'm planning to take her out to see them as soon as she finishes her thesis."

"Ettinger, or rather Herman Lester, had a smooth operation going," Elliot said. "He and his wife were not the only ones involved. We have indictments coming down for nearly a dozen more individuals. But I have to take my hat off to Jasmine for putting a lot of the pieces together."

Jasmine lowered her head. "Once I saw so many similarities between Dr. Ettinger and Dr. Lester, the time period and location and how one person ceased to exist and the other started, everything kinda fell into place from there."

"Excellent job, Jasmine," Jean said.

"I'll need everyone's final report in ten days. Try to do it as soon as possible as details tend to dim." She took off her glasses, a clear indication that the meeting was over.

Everyone stood and began to file out. Ashley was the last to leave. She waited until she was the only one in the room besides Jean.

"Forget something, Ashley?" Jean asked without looking up.

Ashley walked back over to Jean's desk. "I need to ask you something."

Jean glanced up.

"Did you know about my family situation? Is that why you assigned me to this case?"

"What's important is that the right people were chosen and the job was done." She waited a beat. "Anything else?"

Ashley pressed her lips together. "No. I guess not. Thank you." She walked toward the door and opened it.

"Oh, and Ashley . . ."

She turned partly around. "Yes."

"If you tell him how you feel, it will change your life."

Ashley's stomach did a three-sixty as she stared into Jean's all-knowing eyes, an instant before she slipped on her red-framed glasses and looked away.

CHAPTER 22

Ashley checked and rechecked the food. She'd looked in the mirror more in the past hour than she had in her entire lifetime. It had taken her nearly a week to get up the nerve and now she wished she had more time.

What if she was wrong? What if Jean was wrong? What if it was too late?

The bell rang and goose bumps ran up and down her arms. She took a long, deep, cleansing breath, squeezed her eyes shut for a moment then walked to the door.

When she saw Elliot standing on the other side, tall, dark, handsome, edible and looking at her as if he missed her as much as she missed him, she wondered why it had taken her so long.

She took his hand and gently pulled him inside. "Thanks for coming."

"I've never been one to turn down a free meal. And from what I can remember . . .

from our time together, you're a pretty good cook."

She stopped short and turned to him. The muscles in her throat worked up and down. "Do you think about us at all?"

His finger reached out and stroked her cheek. "All the time." The deep timbre of his voice reached inside to that empty place in her soul and filled it.

Her eyes glided over his face, recommitting every inch of it to memory.

"I love you, Ashley. I love you with all my heart. You gave me a reason to want to live again, really live life. To feel again, to want someone in my life that matters, who was there out of desire and not necessity. I've been going crazy these past weeks. I never knew how empty my life was until you weren't in it."

"I love you, Elliot Morgan," she said with all the eagerness and passion that had lived within her for months. "And I don't care if you want to travel to the moon. I want to be with you." There, she'd said it and she was certain that she'd never said anything more true.

He kissed her then — long, deep and sweet and she willingly gave of herself to him. The explosion of their need for each other made them dizzy with desire.

Elliot slowly broke the kiss, leaving Ashley trembling in his embrace. "Marry me, Ashley," he said in an almost urgent whisper. "Travel with me, wake with me, sleep with me, be my friend, my lover, my reflection." He dug in the front pocket of his jeans and took out a diamond ring set in white gold. He held it in front of her. "I didn't come for the free meal. I came to claim my woman."

Ashley's eyes filled with tears of absolute joy. "Yes, yes, yes."

She knew that the road ahead wouldn't be easy, but it would be full of excitement and adventure. With Elliot by her side, and her family united, there wasn't any challenge that she couldn't face.

As she rested in the warmth and security of Elliot's arms, she smiled and silently thanked Jean for knowing just what she needed.

ABOUT THE AUTHOR

Donna Hill began writing novels in 1987. Since then she has published more than forty titles, which include full-length novels and novellas. She easily moves from romance to erotica, horror, comedy and women's fiction. Two of her novels and one novella were adapted for television.

Donna has received numerous awards for her body of work including the *RT Book Reviews* Career Achievement Award, and she is the first recipient of the Trailblazer Award. She currently teaches writing at the Frederick Douglass Creative Arts Center. Donna lives in Brooklyn with her family. Visit her Web site at www.donnahill.com.